Dark EclipsE

RISE OF AN ERA
BOOK
I

BY
CHRISTOPHER M. SALAS

Published by One Level Higher Publishing Company, Longmont, Colorado.

ISBN: 978-0-9785279-3-8
Library of Congress Control Number: 2008924645

Printed in the United States of America

This book is a work of Fiction. Places, events, and situations in this book are purely Fictional and any resemblance to actual persons, living or dead, is coincidental.

Printed in the United States of America

ACKNOWLEDGMENT

First and foremost to GOD for being the guide through the '*Eclipse*'; my dad; my mom & stepdad; Miko, Andromeda, & Piper Salas; Mason Utico; Author photo: Challa Lowry (Touch Of Light Photography); Cover and illustrations: Ethan Wenberg (Squid Works) and Neffra Matthews; Julian & Sandy Sandoval; Elsie, Janice, Rosalie, Isaiah, & Tara Salas; Juanita Mayer; Fred, Maria, & Daniel Cortez; Jeremy & Kellie Cortez; Augustine Jr. & Josie Salas; Pam, Tom, & Jeff McCloy; Matt & Dawn Jensen; Steve, Gayla, & Tim Jensen; Garry, Gloria, & Adom Johnson; Manuel Montiel; Clara Sandoval; Frank & Virginia Sandoval; Sam, Tim, Ed & Pam Webb; Fred, Erlinda, Nicole & Caylene Romaro; Fred & Joan Romaro; Paula, Ron, Brian, & Joshuah Rossetti; Donna & Gary Thiel; Margaret Cruz; Michael & Johnny Merasevik; Cory Esterling; Nana & Pa Bates; Stacey Vowell; Jennifer Riegle; Leo, Barbara, Karly, Adam, & Diane Trujillo; Tony, Dee, & Jessica Molica; Rudy, Charlotte, & Charlotte Sandoval; Georgia, Monique, & Gina Archuleta; Ruben & Martha Sandoval; Daniel & Mellissa Sandoval; Eloy & Heather Sandoval; Rose & Rusty Keaver; Sophie & Chavo Escoto; Joann & Russ Vandenburg; Sensei Lloyd Garcia; Sifu Kerry

Cantrell; Sensei Berry Bernstien; Grant Stephens; Paul Forsthoff; Colorado Springs Street Division; Joe Meridith; Matt Wilson; Jay Griffin; Matt Ziggler; Joe Wagner; Amy & Sean Vowell; Renee Lanning; Linda & Charles Gorham; Nathan & Michelle Roger; Heather Scott; Kris Beatty; Nancy Mayer; Mitzi Mayer; Janice Dickerson; Chuck Mayer; Frank, Alice, & Frank Martinez; Katrina Sandoval; The Rivera Family; Sangre De Cristo Hospice (for the support of my dad); Fred & Roseanna Vigil; Nikki Medina Williams; Kristi Cox; Roy Vasquez; Doc & Diane Cahill; Cecelia Metheney; Dijon Dike; Ken Beaver & Family; Dawn, Samantha, & Patrick Tracey; and last but not least, to those who had doubt.

INTRODUCTION

It's been ten years since the odd story of the *Dark Eclipse* presented itself to me. I knew that it could not be told in one book, but needed to be in three books. At first this story became a screenplay that a friend of mine (Mason Utico) helped co-write. A year later, I moved away and I decided that it would be a good idea to write this story in a trilogy, and then later into a screenplay. There were many changes that had to be done and it was a long and enduring process, and may I not forget, very frustrating. However, to my surprise, it finally all came together. I'm now along for the ride. And the ride I'm having is like the one you the reader are on; the *Dark Eclipse* tale is telling me its story as I write it. I have found that when telling a story, no matter how strange it might be, it all comes from within the heart, mind, and soul. And when it does, it reveals pieces of me, like within certain characters I see my hopes and fears, and in some cases, similar circumstances that I have experienced. However, the real moral of this story is mainly about the good and the evil in humankind. Some of you may even relate to a character or two. I may never know, but if this story gives you enjoyment, then I did my job as a writer.

Perhaps someday there will be other *Dark Eclipse* adventures to follow, but who knows? All I know is that you have the beginning of the *Dark Eclipse* universe in your hands, and you have given me the time to present to you what I have worked for... and I thank you. Enjoy!

The Author-

For My Grandmothers,
Elsie Salas & Juanita Mayer
&
In Loving Memory of My Dad and Grandmother,
Michael Salas
&
Juanita Mayer

To My Sexy Jitsu,
Thank you for who you are.
you are truly irreplaceable!!
I Love you. muah!!

ThE BeginninG

"The future holds a great and terrible threat that will raise its ugly head in the shape of darkness, a threat that will affect us all, and worlds to come."

-Manduurin survivor of the Eclipse

The Fall of Bytiluna

The fall of Bytiluna was discovered underground in the charred ruins of the pyramids of Cydonia in an arm-length capsule that protected it from being burned beyond recognition. It was then sent to Earth to be identified and translated by five of Earth's most respected encryptors: Dr. Lena Schweizer [Germany], Dr. Demetrio Ruiz [Spain], Dr. Matthew F. Bennett [United Kingdom], Dr. Yumi Katsukawa [Japan], Dr. Geddes Macfie [Scotland], and Michael B. Evans [United States], respectively. The translation took seven years.

Note from the translators: After spending countless hours with this remarkable text, we all agree that the language, although undoubtedly extra-terrestrial, is very similar to the Hamo-Semitic language of the Middle Kingdom of Ancient Egypt. That is not to say that the linguistic and semantic elements are identical, only that they are strangely similar. Moreover, the paper was carbon dated at 252 years old. *Pages three to seven of the manuscript, containing chapters three through five, are lost. Therefore, the extant text starts on page one and then continues on page six. In many places, certain verses within the following chapters were unsalvageable due to their charred condition, and are thus deemed throughout as "missing."* The content is very fragmented;

nevertheless, its historical significance is inestimable. Sadly, the following is the only history humanity has of the Chlordon, the mysterious figures from the star system Bytiluna and the fathers of the Eclipse.

Chapter 1.

The entreaty of the teacher the first son of the king

...by the will of good, to the people of hope and to those faithful to the standard, whomever you may be, herein is a testament to the history of a wise and sacred civilization that perished before it could give account to the hazards that walk with wisdom when wisdom walks into war.

Chapter 2.

A time of harmony

Vs 12. Twelve centuries of serenity, whereby the moons of Bytiluna rejoiced for innocence, for hope, and for wisdom.

Vs 13. Twelve hundred years of [warmth] without cold, of harvests without famine, of bodies without rot...

Vs 14. Twelve centuries of harmony, whereby a proud civilization prospered without the weapons of war.

Vs 15. Twelve hundred years of peace, for [peace] was the standard... (Verses 16-34 missing)

Chapter 6.

From heavens the murderer comes

Vs 35. Then he came, descending from the heavens of Bytiluna with hissing minions - the conjurer, the king of Icubin.

Vs 37. …ushering in a new era [of] dread … (*Missing*)

Vs 41. Morgmordeus-Demonixa was his name… (*Missing*)

Vs 42. …and [Morgmordeus] the murderer reigned with the sword of tyranny. (*Missing*)

Vs 49. Yes it is true, that the echoes of goodness were swallowed by the throat of evil…by that terrible void in his neck.

Vs 50. (*Missing*) Scores of planets splintered; [many] more crushed… (*Missing*)

Vs 51. (*Missing*)...the galaxy likewise fell under his boot heel. Soon the rest of Andromeda would succumb… (*Verses 52-64 missing*)

Chapter 7.

Bearers of the standard

Vs 65. …only one race resisted, defying Morgmordeus and the new era, the Chlordon: the pioneers of the charted systems of Bytiluna, emissaries of Andromeda, and [the] bearers of the standard of peace.

Vs 66. Thus war was declared and raged for nine solar years…

(*Verses 67-82 missing*)

Chapter 8.

The blackest of hate

Vs 83. (*missing*)…the Chlordon, clinging to minute

victories in battles that ravaged [their] cities, decimated their populations, and weakened their natural resources, held steadfast.

Vs 84. However, with each twilight the sun dwindled, as the expanse from which it breathes in life so that it may breathe out light, became ever more infected with Morgmordeus's hate.

Vs 86. Behold, his hate contaminated that expanse, and then the sky above them, and then the oceans around [them], and then the rivers among them, and then the soil beneath them, and then many of the hearts within them.

Vs 89. Yes, it is true, that the translucent expanse, and the turquoise sky, and the blue oceans and rivers, and the ashen soil, and the red blood in the hearts of several of the Chlordon turned black, and thereby turned [brother] against brother, father against mother, and… (*Verses 90-92 missing*)

Vs 93. …their democracy toppled, their cities lamed, their temples desecrated, their covenants broken, [their] hopes burned at the stake with the horizon, the first Son of the King and the four physicists of the Glataaga council used their knowledge to build a weapon unlike any other [in the] cosmos, a weapon that could eradicate evil in the blink of an eye.

Vs 94. Yes it is true; the Eclipse was born to meet that hate in the abyss, and to drown it there (*Verses 95-100 missing*)

Chapter 9.

The end of an evil era

Vs 101. Knowing that a single confrontation could end

the war, the Chlrodon sought out Morgmordeus.
Vs 102. Hearing from a spy who gave his life for the cause that Morgmordeus had returned to his home planet, the Chlordon gathered [their] remaining forces and headed for Icubin.
Vs 103. The battle lasted for eight long solar days in the skies of Icubin.
Vs 104. On the ninth day, the enemies of peace had finally weakened… good now [had] the upper hand.
Vs 105. "Finish it!" The words were said, and it was done. The weapon was launched. A flash of blackness [hit] the planet…
Vs 106. Icubin was eclipsed and so was the evil era… (*107 missing*)
Vs 108 …And goodness was then restored. (*Verses 109-110 missing)*

Chapter 10.

The scrolls of Tranquility

Vs 111. After the Great War of Bytiluna, the Chlordon wrote the encryption formulas to the Eclipse on scrolls called *Tranquility* and [hid] their most sacred place, the Yrmid temple on the planet Xom in the star system Teelin Reticuli.
Vs 112. Only the first son of the King and the four founding fathers of the Eclipse could enter the temple. (*Verses 113-117 missing*)

Chapter 11.

The ascension of the Dark Prince

Vs 118. Two solar years had passed since the Great War. Icubin recovered its losses and the Chlordon returned

to [their] peaceful existence. But all of that would end, again.
Vs 119. First it was the calm; the evil [had] a new name, then it was the peacefulness; the coming of a second era, and then it was the goodness; the Dark Prince had risen, and his name was Carnmassicre-Oroan, second son of Morgmordeus-Demonixa.
Vs 120. With his sister Minda-Proserpine by his right hand, he became more powerful than his father… (*Verses 121-123 missing*)
Vs 124. Carnmassicre conjured an army that was so impregnable they would bring the second era to an uprise. This army was known as the Demonixa, the demolition hammer of the prince of evil.
Vs 125. Technology with evil, [they were] an unimaginable combination.
Vs 126. Shortly after the uprise Carnmassicre sent his minion spies on a mission to the star system Teelin Reticuli, to raid the planet Xom and retrieve the Eclipse [encryptions] from the Yrmid temple.
Vs 127. …the mission was successful.
Vs 128. Soon Carnmassicre replicated the weapon [that] destroyed his world two solar years ago and that would soon destroy the enemy of the Demonixa.
Vs 129. Carnmassicre turned all his hate toward the Chlordon.

Chapter 12.

The day of punishment

Vs 130. The day was peaceful [with the] gentle breeze that felt of soft goodness as it touched the horizon as the smiling sun shined.

Vs 131. …came without warning from the east, and the west, and the north, and the south.
Vs 132. The sky [was] swallowed with moving blackness [and] the color of blood accented each ship in an outline.
Vs 133. In the shape of crescent moons the demolition-hammer fell with the presence of fear and a promise of a future of sadness.
Vs 134. They were the black angels of the Demonixa, the deliverers of hate; they were the Wraith…
Vs 135. Xom's surface shook from the sounds [as the] Wraith drew closer to the it's surface (verse 136 missing)
Vs 137. It was the day of punishment through the eyes of the second era. (*Verse 138 missing*)
Vs 139. The devastation was complete…
Vs 140. The Eclipse was launched [into] Xom's orbit and ended…
Vs 141. There were no known survivors.

Chapter 13.

Bloodline

Vs 142. Half a solar day later, the Demonixa invaded [the planet] Egypuun, also in the Reticuli system.
Vs 143. Egypuun was inhabited by a race of beings that [were from] a distant bloodline to the Chlordon. They were the Manduurin [and] they too had the Eclipse knowledge.
Vs 144. Like the Chlordon the Manduurin had written the encryptions in a temple wall called *Tranquility…* (*Verses 145-148 missing*)
Vs 149. The Manduurin tried to evacuate, but Wraiths

swarmed [like] locusts through the smoke-filled sky, destroying any ship that tried to escape.
Vs 150. "Suuccttuurra Viivviiddoodda!" The words were spoken in deep summons... and the Egypuun soil gave birth to the bitter nectar of the conjuring: the eyeless beasts known as the Noraphamara. The demons that damn the soul [by the] desecration of the forbidden fruit of the flesh, and the Godless children of the evil prince.
Vs 151. Behold, the Noraphamara arose with spine raising shrieks and brought death [at] command.
Vs 152. …satisfied that the soil had been saturated in blood, the Noraphamara dissipated into the ground. (*Verses 153-154 missing*)
Vs 155. After the Manduurin ships reached space, the Eclipse was on its way to the planet's surface. The Manduurin knew that there were no hopes in saving their planet [from] destruction… (*Verses 156-158 missing*)
Vs 159. In a blink of an eye, Egypuun's fate had come. By diverting in all directions the nine remaining ships escaped [with] minor damage, they then fled to the spiral arms of the Milky Way galaxy to where they [may] find refuge...
Vs 160. …only 28,000 Manduurin survived.

Chapter 14.

The coming of a second era

Brethren, to those who [have] ears, for the will of good, I have testified unto the truth. And for those who [will] listen to that truth, I [ask] thee: Will there be a future or not?

THE CORPS

DEMONIXA

PART ONE

ThE MissoN

-1-

Planet, Kliia: 5/5/2090

Milky Way Galaxy: Gleera Star System

In a helpless mind filled with indignation, a man lay in a terrible enigmatic state. *Heal my wounds.* His eyes twirled underneath the lids. *Please forgive me.* His head abruptly turned side-to-side. *I can't feel my heart.* His fingers and toes slightly twitched. *I cannot speak; I cannot breathe.*

"Max!" A girl cried out, strapped to the floor with a set of claw-like hands clamped to her arms. Two Noraphamara cackled in pleasure as they watched the girl's agony. In a quick flashover like a slide to a picture show, a tall, woman-like being stood over Max with her sword held at mid-level. "Baptized in blood." she said, and then thrust her double-edged sword into Max's pregnant wife's stomach.

"Emily!" Max cried.

The figure resembled a well-defined female with snow-white hair wrapped in a ponytail resting at her right shoulder and tipped with a blade. Her sapphire eyes were slightly slanted, her body color resembled black ash. "Now sadness comes unto thee and falls at the feet upon the unborn." Her voice lingered throughout the room, like an echo swimming through a dark cave.

He awoke, covered with the cold sweat from the shock and pain of a never ending nightmare. The blood and cries permeated his mind as it intertwined with the new day. *Will it end?* Time will heal. *It's been eight years.* But time will heal.

Unexpected knocks at the door caused Max to draw his custom Glock .45 Viper pistol that lay at his side next to the sweat-sopped pillow. Wiping the caked salt from his hair and stubble face with his forearm, he tried to wake up. The knock repeated. "You've got the wrong room. Leave me alone." The knock continued. He got up from the bed, walked to the door and looked through the peephole. He noticed a tall, light blue colored alien in a military uniform holding a sliver briefcase. He opened the door. "Major," the alien saluted.

"I'm retired," he said.

"Sir?" the alien murmured.

"Come in soldier," Max said.

The alien entered the room. "Thank you, sir." The alien nodded. He placed the briefcase on a table that was catty-corner of the room. He then opened the case by touching an insignia that was at the top of it. The opened case revealed a blank screen and multiple computer keys at the base of it. The alien pushed a couple of keys and then stood to the side of the table at attention. The screen revealed a transmission from a five-star general in his mid-fifties. "Greetings, Maxwell."

"General Kipling," Max returned.

"We have a mission for you," Kipling said.

Max placed his pistol on the bar. "Would you like a drink, soldier?" he offered.

"No thank you, sir," the alien said.

Max picked up a half-filled bottle of Gin, his mind still disoriented from his nightmare; then poured some into a glass with ice. "Suit yourself... down the hatch." He tipped the glass up to his mouth and swallowed. "So, what's on your mind, General?"

"The Corps needs you."

"I'm no longer in the Corps, General," Max interrupted.

"The counsel is aware of that; they will compensate you for the job," Kipling said.

Max poured again, then swallowed. "Go on."

"What do you know about the Eclipse?" Kipling asked.

"Not much. Why?"

"We received a deep space transmission from the planet Xissba, which, of course, over half the planet is in Demonixa order warning us that Carnmassicre is going to send one of his minions back through time to eliminate the four physicists that replicated the Eclipse..." Kipling paused briefly.

Max lit his cigar. "I'm sorry," he said. "Back through time?"

"That's right." The computer screen cleared Kipling's image, then revealed a picture of a bluish transparent sphere. The general appeared in view in the upper right-hand side of the screen. "The Polaris type two sphere. Like its older sister, the Polaris type one, it possesses the capability to create an event horizon through space. Yet, the type two can tear holes in the space-time strand. Its main function is time travel."

"I think you need to get out more and lay off the *Twilight Zone* reruns." Max took two puffs from his cigar. "With all do respect, General, I have no time for games."

Kipling folded his hands together. "We need you for this mission, Maxwell."

"Brilliant minds at work, I see." Max took another drag. "If I accepted this mission, what would I have to do?"

"You would have to go back in time to Earth in Egypt and stop the Demonixa from assassinating the physicists," Kipling said.

"The main lab underneath the great pyramids?" Max asked.

"Yes, that's right."

"Do you know how far back they've gone, what month, what day?"

"August 5, 2078."

"Twelve years. Sounds simple, but what if something goes wrong with the mission?"

Kipling leaned back in his chair. "You're a highly intelligent man, Maxwell. We're not the only race that possesses the Eclipse technology. The Demonixa were the first to posses its power."

"At least that's what we were told," Max interrupted.

"Look, you were an excellent soldier, Maxwell, and you're the perfect man for the job."

"I'm a bounty hunter now, General, not a hero. Get Anom Lawrence. He's the man you want for the job."

Max stood up and headed for the door, then opened it. “Thanks, General, but no thanks. I didn’t get out of this shit to turn around and jump head first right back into it,” Max said.

The computer screen cleared again, but this time the picture was not as appeasing to Max’s eyes.

“Do you remember her? She’s Carnmassicre’s second in command as well as his most loyal minion…”

Max remembered, and his heart remembered, and his nerves wallowed in tremors. His palms itched and he knew why. *But it’s been eight years.* Max slowly closed the door to the room. “Continue, General,” he said.

“Minda will be the one that will be sent in time, and I know that you’ve confronted her in the past. That’s why we think you’re the perfect candidate.”

How does that make me the perfect candidate? Max thought. *I know why. I owe the bitch.* “I don’t have much of a choice here, do I?”

“You’re not in the Corps, so you have a choice,” the general assured.

“I used to have a choice, but not now.”

Kipling’s image appeared back on the screen. “We will assign as many soldiers as you need. And like I said before, the Corps will fully compensate you for your troubles.”

Max took one last drag of his cigar and crushed the smoldering tip in the ashtray, then exhaled. “No, keep your money. I’ll go alone. Just give me what I need for my mission and the names of the four physicists, and we’ll call it good.”

“We’ll install the Polaris as soon as possible. When you get to your ship, you will be meeting with a

Manduurin physicist named Tillin-Vii and he will brief you on the sphere," Kipling said.

"When will I be leaving?" Max asked.

The general looked at his watch. "09:00."

"I still have time before I report." Max sat down in a chair that was near the bed and leaned back with his hands folded behind his head. "Is there anything else, General?"

"Yes, watch your ass," he said, and then stood up from his desk chair. "Good luck and Godspeed, Maxwell. Kipling, out."

"Luck is an overrated luxury."

Shortly after the transmission ended, the alien closed the briefcase. "Sir," he said, saluting. He then headed for the door with the case in hand, without another word.

Hours later, the Vortex stood brave and strong while the physicists worked on new modifications inside a cleared out aircraft hanger, deep inside the Kiooma Mountains. The ship's wings were slightly inverted, as well as the four other wings at the tail end of the ship. The body of the ship looked about fifty yards in length, and about two stories in height, with its cockpit tucked into its front upper body like a turtle's head tucked in its shell. The outer hull of the Vortex displayed numerous scorch marks due to space derbies and blaster grazing.

Max entered the hanger fully prepared. He wore a thin, black, alien in origin, fabric spacesuit with thin black chest armor and matching boots that had splits between the toes. He also sported black gloves with a silver Corps symbol on the back of the hand, two custom black .45 Glock Vipers in their shoulder holsters, and a ninja-to-sword sheathed to his back with square hilt, the handle wrapped in leather. The sword itself dated back to the sixteenth century. Finally, underneath his right arm he carried a black and silver helmet with two black eye lenses. The helmet had four types of vision: normal, ultraviolet, infra-red, and scope (binocular affect), as well as its own life support system. As Max walked through the hanger, he noticed 16 soldiers lined up fully armed, and seven physicists that were working inside and outside of the Vortex. He stopped his stride for a brief moment. "Reporting for duty, Major," A familiar man's voice said. Max looked over his shoulder.

"Anom!" He said in surprise, then smiled and shook his hand.

"It's good to see you, my friend..." He gave Max a hug and a pat on the back. "It's been a long time. What, two or three years?"

Max smiled. "It's been a while."

They both walked towards the Vortex. "By the way, what brings you here? I heard that you made Commander," Max said.

"That's right. I'm the new first officer of the U.S.S. Mayflower. Besides, when I heard that Major Leer, a good buddy I might add, had a space time continuum gig, I had to come."

Max smirked. "It's been my childhood dream, let me tell you."

"The truth is that I suggested you for the job," he said.

"Remind me to cut you from my Christmas list," Max said.

"I think instead of a bounty hunter you should be a comedian," Lawrence suggested.

"No, seriously I'm cutting you."

A Manduurin physicist approached Max and Anom as the two continued their conversation.

"You must be Major Leer," the Manduurin said.

"It never fails. Yes, I'm Maxwell Leer, and you must be, Tillin-Vii. Right?"

The Manduurin nodded. "Come with me," he insisted.

"So, what's up with my ship?"

"It's fine, sir. We are in the final stages now. We are double-checking our work as we speak."

They entered into the Vortex inner hull. Lawrence tapped his knuckles on the wall of the ship. "This brings back memories, Max," he said as they entered the engine room. Tillin began to explain the Polaris type two and all its functions. Lawrence watched the other physicists while they double-checked every modification.

"So, Doc, what will I come to expect as I'm shooting through time?" Max asked.

"Come with me to the cockpit," Tillin said.

As they entered the cockpit, Tillin explained the newly added controls to Max.

"Is there an instruction booklet with the sphere, so if anything goes wrong?" Lawrence said as Max gave him an odd look.

"Hey, good friends are hard to come by, you know," Anom said.

"If you have any questions about the type two, it will supply you with the information."

"Any questions?" Max said.

"Yeah, anything."

"So, can I ask it who shot Kennedy?" Max asked.

"No, it can't do that, nor can it tell you how many licks it takes to get to the center of a tootsie pop," Tillin remarked.

"Do you think the type two can read my future?" Lawrence asked.

"Yeah, and it might say to give up on Rhiannon."

"Gentleman, can we focus?" Tillin said.

"Or it might say not to," Lawrence whispered.

"The first thing..." Tillin began, as another physicist handed him a mini digital clipboard.

"Sir, all modifications are ready," the physicist confirmed.

Tillin nodded. "As I was saying, the first thing that will happen is that there will be a brief bright light that forms into what is called a white hole. That white hole will suck your ship into what is known as the event stream. That event stream will form into a black hole, and that black hole will become time. Do you understand?"

"In the King's English, Doc." Max returned.

"We don't have time for the King's English, but don't worry, the type two is already programmed with the date of where you need to be."

"Has this type two been tested?" Max asked.

"Yes sir, we've tested it numerous times," Tillin confirmed, "but this is the only type two in existence, a prototype."

"So, how did Carnmessicre get ahold of this technology?" Max asked.

"We have no idea. We may never know. All we know is that the Demonixa have taken the time travel technology, just like the Eclipse," Tillin said.

"Is there anything else, Doc?" Max asked.

"Have you been to Earth?"

"Only my first year in the academy."

Tillin handed Max a digital atlas of Earth. "You will need this," he said. "The atlas is programmed with blueprints of the main lab and the great pyramids."

"Thanks, Doc."

"Lift off is in five minutes, sir," Tillin said.

"Ten-four, Doc," Max said. "Just one more question, Doc."

"Yes?"

"When I come back, if I do, how will the council know about any changes that have accrued? Assuming that there will be any changes to the time line."

"The sphere will keep a log of your journey and it will also keep track of any changes that may be in effect. The Polaris will be safe going in and out of each time line," Tillin ended, as he left the ship.

Lawrence pulled out a 1947 penny in a clear coin case from the inside of his black military jacket and handed it to Max. "For good luck," he said.

"I can't take this; it was your great grandfather's," Max said.

"If it makes you feel better, you could give it back when you return. It's given me good luck when I needed it. Besides, my friend, you need all the luck you can get."

"Luck is an overrated luxury," Max said as he stuffed the antique penny inside his space suit jacket pocket. "For your grandfather," he said.

"By the way, you still owe me two snake bite shots for the bet that you lost." Lawrence smirked. "Remember?"

"Unfortunately for you, I do," Max said.

"Oh, before I forget. A going away gift." He pulled out a package wrapped in brown paper and handed it to Max.

"My birthday is four months off."

"Just open it," Anom said.

Max opened the package expecting an old academy prank like fake vomit, a fake finger, or just maybe a piece of half-eaten chewing gum. Instead it was a mint first addition copy of H.G. Wells' *The Time Machine*.

Max grinned. "Of course, only you could think of something like this."

"Do you like it?"

"I do. But I don't have time to read it. No pun intended. Where did you find this?" Max asked as he flipped through the crisp pages of the book. "I'm sure it wasn't easy to find."

"I found it in an old antique shop on Earth." Lawrence folded his arms behind him. "I also purchased some *Spider-Man* comics. Good issues by the way."

Max looked up at Lawrence as he closed his book. "How many comics do you have now?"

"Well over 1,741 and growing."

Tillin entered the ship once again. "Sir, it's time."

"Well, my friend, look me up when you come back."

Max nodded. "I will. And thanks for the book."

"Don't mention it. Maybe you can read it when you retire."

"I keep trying to do that, you know," Max said.

"What, read?"

Max smiled.

“Take care,” Anom said while approaching the door of the Vortex.

“Hey Anom, do you really want me to ask this thing about Rhiannon?”

“No, but you can ask it about the tootsie pop.” Anom smiled and walked out the door.

Later the Vortex’s gangway closed. After, the ship raised itself from the ground, the three landing feet tucked into the ship’s hull as it slowly moved out from the hanger. The thrusters engaged with a loud roar and the ship exited the Kliia atmosphere, and flew into space.

-2-

Planet, Earth: 8/5/2078
Milky Way Galaxy: Delta-1 Star System

Somewhere on the border of New Mexico and Arizona, miles away from the nearest town, a young and promising astrophysicist named Sara Manning pressed her eye against her telescope, observing the eight moons of Neptune, Naiad, Thalassa, Despina, Galatea, Larissa, Triton, Proteus, and Nereid.

The first was the moon Triton. She focused on the sparkling ball and smiled. “There you are,” she said in a mild Scottish accent. As the telescope zoomed in on the alien moon, the young astronomer reached down to her lens kit and picked up a long scope with a thicker lens. She softly hummed along with the song *Dream Weaver*, which was playing on her mini CD player. A grin filled her face when she focused closer to Triton’s surface. “Only if Father were here to see it,” she said.

She then reached for her notebook filled with notes and diagrams. Next, she reached for the pen that was tucked in her right breast pocket and jotted down her hypotheses on Triton. She then dropped her notebook down and continued to view the other moons.

Soon after, Sara packed her gear into a large, black, hard leather case, and then packed her mini CD player in a green backpack that had her Scottish family crest at the back end of it near the zipper. She then placed her bags in her newly restored blue 1999 Jeep with its top down and its roll cage exposed. She looked up briefly at the stars while reaching for her keys. A faint sound of compressed air mixed with what sounded like aircraft thrusters echoed at a nearby hill, approximately fifty yards away. *There must be spacecraft testing near?* she thought. *I should check it out.*

When she approached the hill where the unfamiliar sound originated, a loud crunch filled the air as rocks from the Earth's surface were being crushed and smothered by something heavy. Sara turned off her headlights as she got closer, and then stopped about fifteen feet away from the hill.

She hiked up the hill as the sounds became louder. Sara peeked her head over a big rock that was near a large cactus. She then noticed a mid-sized star ship and her eyes widened. "What in God's name?" she said.

The Vortex's gangway opened. She tucked her head closer to the rock. Only her eyes and the top of her head were exposed.

Max walked out of the ship and into the night air, but Sara could not make out who it was, nor could she tell if the stranger was friendly or not. She watched him looking up at the horizon and then at what seemed to be some kind of scanner.

Sara quickly crawled to the other side of the rock,

not knowing that there was a cliff just thirteen inches away. "OH, SHIT!" she blurted out while trying to brace for the fall. Luckily, the cliff was only a small drop to the bottom.

Max quickly drew his .45 from its holster and pointed it in the direction of the unknown noise. "Show yourself!" he said. His helmet automatically activated its infra-red system. "Come out and show yourself."

"Ouch," Sara gasped, as she pulled out the thorns that had penetrated her forearm and it began to bleed. "That's just great," she said.

"Identify yourself now!" he said while keeping his weapon aimed.

Sara walked closer to the stranger, yet she was slightly hesitant. "Are you lost, stranger?" she asked.

He holstered his weapon. "Didn't your mother ever tell you, never talk to strangers?"

"Ouch," she mumbled to herself as she pulled the last of the thorns from her elbow. "I'm twenty-six, not a child," she said as she patted the dirt from her jeans. "Besides, you look lost, stranger." She couldn't see the man's eyes or his face, only dark empty eye pieces. "You must be one of the soldiers I've been hearing on the news?"

"I don't think so," Max murmured.

Sara walked up to the Vortex with curious intentions. "Boy, look at all the scorch marks. There must be something big happening up there, isn't there?"

"Up where?" He kept scanning his atlas.

"I'm not stupid, stranger." She looked back at Max. "My father is a physicist for the Corps. I have a good idea of what's going on."

Max quickly turned to face her. "What's his name?"

She looked at him oddly. "Seth Manning. Why?"

"Was he stationed at Giza?"

"Tell me, is there something wrong with my father?" she asked.

"Where is he?" Max said sternly.

She began to panic. "I think he told me that he had a big project with three other physicists. I believe he was stationed there, but I'm not sure."

Max located Egypt with his atlas and then rushed to his ship.

"Hey, is my father okay?" Sara firmly gripped Max's arm like a clamping vice. "Is he in trouble?" Her eyes were fixed on Max's eye pieces.

"Your father will be fine." Max began to walk up the gangway.

"I'm going with you," Sara said.

"I don't think so, girlie. You're staying here."

"If my father is in danger, I need to be with him."

"I don't have time for games, girlie. If you want to see your father alive, I need you to stay here. You would be a liability..."

"I'm not a liability," Sara said.

"Stay here and your daddy-o will be just fine; I'll make sure of it."

Sara stood at the foot of the gangway lost in thought as Max entered his ship. The ship lifted off the ground as the gangway began to close. Sara jumped up on the gangway just before its departure. The ship's thrusters roared into the distance towards an echoing void.

Inside the Vortex, Max placed his helmet on the

copilot chair next to his sword. He charted his course to Egypt into the Vortex's database, and then activated the autopilot. He then walked out of the cockpit and headed to the arsenal room.

Sara poked her head around the corner of the hallway with her hands gripping the edge. *What in hell have I gotten myself into,* she thought.

After creeping down the hallway, she noticed a door from a distance away on the right. When she reached the door, she looked to see if the stranger was about, but he wasn't to be found. The door opened wit out warning, causing her to jump back. The room was dark, but that did not stop her curiosity. As she entered the room, the overhead lights activated and the door slid shut behind her.

Max struck a match and started to light his cigar, suddenly he noticed a faint noise coming from the arsenal room. He extinguished the match before the flame reached the tip of the cigar. He drew his .45 and aimed it at the door. The door opened and Sara screamed at the top of her lungs. Max withdrew his weapon. "Dammit, to hell...?"

"I'm sorry, but I'm not going to just live my life and pretend that nothing's wrong."

"Now I have no choice but to take you with me. I don't have time to take you back," he said. "But you'll have to stay in the ship, no if's, and's or but's about it, girlie."

"I can take care of myself, stranger. I think I could help with your mission or whatever you need to do to solve our problem," she said.

"I don't think so, you're staying on the ship."

"Look, I know how to shoot a gun."

"Anyone can shoot a gun."

"Would you stop calling me girlie. I have a name, you know."

"Listen, girlie, I don't have time to argue with you about this."

"Sara," she said.

"What?"

"My name is Sara."

"Look, Sara..."

"Do you have a name, or should I just keep calling you stranger?"

"Max."

"Just Max?"

"Just Max," he replied.

"Well, it's nice to meet you, Max."

He gave a faint smile.

"Besides the cute smile, what's with the antique weapons?"

"I like antiques; they're reliable."

"Yeah, but they're fragile," Sara said.

"Whatever. You're one to talk."

"What?"

"When I was scanning the horizon, my sensors picked up that song you were humming," Max returned.

"Song?" Sara asked, slightly embarrassed.

"*Dream Weaver*. Talk about a fragile antique."

"If you keep giving me shit, I'll hum *Knights in White Satin*."

"Is there a hidden message in that title?"

"Never mind," she said and pointed to a silver box that had Japanese calligraphy on the lid. "What does that mean?"

"It's just a label for what's in the box."

"Well, what's in the box?"

"You ask too many questions," he said while handing her an extra black space suit and a hooded mask with tinted eye lenses. "Here, take this and change quickly."

"What's this for?"

"It's to keep you from getting all scuffed up."

"It looks like a Ninja costume."

"It's not a Ninja costume," Max rebutted.

"Yes, but do you agree that it looks like a Ninja costume?"

"I have only three rules. Rule number one: do whatever I say. Rule number two: follow rule number one. And rule number three: don't ask me about my rules."

"Why do you have to have rules?"

"You just broke rule number three," Max said.

"Well, do you really need rules two and three?"

"What?"

"Well, aren't they kind of redundant?"

"What?"

"You know, like irregardless."

"What?"

"Well..."

"Okay," he interrupted. "One and one rule only: do whatever I say!"

"Did you take rule making 101 at DU?"

"What's DU?"

"You know, Dictator University?" Sara smirked and then left the room to change clothes.

What the hell was I thinking bringing her long, he thought.

Max reached into one of the ammo drawers and pulled out two boxes of .12 gauge shotgun shells. He then grabbed a black waste ammo belt with Velcro straps attached to the ends to store the shells in.

Minutes later, Sara entered the room carrying her jeans and shirt with the hood on top. She placed them on the floor and tied her hair in a ponytail with a rubber band that she had in her jeans' pocket.

He handed her the belt with the .12 gage shells and a black vest shield.

"What's this for?"

He handed her a loaded pump action .12 gauge shot gun with a Velcro ammo strap at the stock of the rifle. "Just in case shit happens, and if it does happen, your chances of missing will be slim."

"Funny." She strapped the vest and the belt on.

Max opened the silver box with the Japanese writing, and a blue light peeked over the edge of the opening.

"What is that?" Sara's eyes glittered from the blue light.

He picked up a crystal blue, liquid nitrogen wrist blaster, and placed it on his left arm. The blue energy weapon formed to Max's lower arm like hot wax. "This is a nitrogen blaster," he said.

"Sounds dangerous," Sara remarked.

The ship's computer alerted Max to his arrival. Without any notice he left the arsenal room and headed for the cockpit. Sara then followed.

In the cockpit, Max resumed manual control of the ship. He looked at his atlas monitor for a brief second for a confirmation status. "Have you ever been to Egypt?" he asked.

"No. Have you?"

"No."

"It looks like a ghost town. Shouldn't there be some sort of activity?"

"You would think."

She checked the shotgun to see if the safety was engaged, then rested it in her arm. "I hope we're not too late, Max."

He looked over his shoulder at her. "I have a feeling that we're not." *And if we are, would I still feel the affects or am I protected by this time change?* he thought.

Not long after, the (Khufu) pyramid's ancient inner structure lay empty except for a somber mix of cryptic smells and aged silence. Max and Sara walked with caution, unsure of what lay ahead. Wooden torches lit the sand-covered hallway, revealing proof of some previous brutal activity. Traces of fresh blood spattered in a blotchy, fan-like pattern were displayed on the walls and the floor of the structure like works of morbid art.

"Well it sure ain't bacon," he said as he lowered his sword, removing the loose skin with his boot.

They only walked a few yards before Sara whispered, "Max, I'm scared."

"Stay close to me."

"What could do this?" Sara asked and moved as close as she could to Max.

"God awful things."

The crimson trail ended at a darkened stairwell that led downward, yet there were no bodies to be found. Sara grabbed a torch from the wall as her hands shook like a smoker suffering from a nicotine fit.

"Sara, are you alright?"

"Y-yes, I'm fine," Sara nodded, then looked back and saw nothing.

"Watch your step." Max's eye pieces turned a shady red color as his helmet activated its infra-red system. He pulled out one of his .45s from the holster. Sara kept the torch between her and the darkness behind her. She frequently looked back to see if they were being followed, but there was no one there.

Max paused as he noticed a shadow of bright light in the distance. "I see light."

"What do you see?" Sara asked.

He didn't say a word.

"Max?"

He then continued down the stairwell to the light. His helmet returned to its normal sight. A faint moan crept in the air and slowly, a muscular slouching shadow moved across the lighted area.

"Max?"

Max pointed the .45 at the shadow. "Whatever happens, stay out of the way. Do you understand?"

The moans became louder as they approached closer. The slouched shadow disappeared. *Noraphamara,* Max thought.

"Someone help me..." a female's voice whimpered. "Help me please."

As they reached the bottom of the stairwell, Max poked his head around the corner of the entrance of the lighted hallway. He saw white tile floors and white walls with five, sliding steel doors; four on the right, and one at the end of the corridor. Four out of the five doors showed evidence of forced entry, like something ripped the steel doors to shreds, but no Noraphamara.

"What did this?" Sara asked

"Extinguish the torch, stay here and don't move till I say," he said before he entered the hallway with his .45 pointed at the shredded doors.

"Be careful," Sara whispered.

The female whimpers became louder and louder, then suddenly ceased as Max approached the first room. He noticed the lights flicker as strands of sparks shot down from the sockets, as well as slimy goop at the shredded tips of the door. *I'm too late,* he thought. Yet Max didn't say a word, knowing that Sara would panic. Max slowly backed away from the door with his .45 pointed.

"Max, what's wrong?"

He waved his hand while keeping his eyes fixed at the door. Sara tucked herself into the shadows with her finger at the trigger. Max looked over at the other entrance while simultaneously returning back to the first. "Help me..." The whimpering voice had returned. "Someone, please help me."

Max slowly walked to the door. "Name and rank," he said sternly.

"Help me," the voice continued, yet the pleads began to fade in cadence with every step that Max took towards the forced entrance.

"I repeat. Name and rank!" Max demanded.

The voice ceased, swallowed by the silence of the undetermined void.

"I repeat one last t..."

A deep growling wheeze crept out from the room. Suddenly a sandy brown muscular beast jumped out and tackled Max, pinning him on his back. The demonic creature slapped the .45 from Max's hand with its long, blood-stained claw. The beast had sharp teeth with thick strands of saliva at the tips of its canines. Its ears contorted into its head. It had no eyes, but a skin-withered covering. The flesh itself looked as if it had suffered severe burns and skin grafts.

Sara screamed when she saw the creature. She pumped and lifted the .12 gauge while heading towards Max and the Noraphamara.

"STAY BACK! DON'T LET IT GET CLOSE TO YOU!" Max struggled.

The beast turned to Sara. "FEESSTTA XOOKKOOD!" it hissed.

"SHIT! RUN!" Max shouted.

Sara's eyes widened and her heart pounded fast and thick. "Max? Maaaaax!" she screamed. The Noraphamara lunged off of Max and at Sara with great speed. The slimy saliva dripped from its teeth as its pointed tongue licked its mouth with pleasure. Sara made a mad dash for the stairs, but it was too late. The demonic beast slammed her to the wall. She grunted with a cough from the impact, then fell limp.

"QOOSSTTA VIILLZ!" the beast chuckled, while its teeth chattered in an appalling click. The smell of corpse from its breath dominated.

Max picked himself up and ran to the beast. He grabbed the creature by its thick neck, then torqued his hips and whipped the Noraphamara over his shoulders. The beast fell like a bag of rocks and landed with a hard thump. "Hurts, doesn't it, you pestilent f...?"

The Noraphamara stood up and howled. It swung its claws at Max's head. Max tucked and parried, then threw a right vertical punch to the creature's abdomen. The beast grunted. He simultaneously threw a left reverse punch to its ribs and ended with a right cross stomp to the creature's knee. The Noraphamara shrieked and fell to its crippled knee.

"Max, behind you!" Sara shouted.

Another creature grabbed Max by the torso and lifted him off the ground while squeezing his ribs. Max repeatedly thrust his elbows at the beast's forearms. When it finally released Max from its arms, Max executed a back kick to the creature's kneecap and the sound of crunching bone echoed through the hallway. He finished by unsheathing his sword and lopping both Noraphamara's heads off. Their corpses twitched as the nerve endings from their severed necks leaked what looked like oil onto the ground. Max wiped off his blade on the arm of his suit and then sheathed it. "Are you alright?"

Sara's eyes didn't blink or move; she was in shock. "Y-yes. Wh-what are they?" her voice trembled.

Max picked up his .45 and holstered it. "Demons. Noraphamara are their names."

"Demons you say?" She was puzzled. "How? I… I'm confused."

"When the Noraphamara rises from the ground and is fully conjured, and I mean flesh and blood, it is no longer supernatural. It becomes mortal."

"Where do they come from?"

"They're summoned by another unworldly force, black magic if you will. Either way, the bastards are easy to kill."

Sara picked up the .12 gauge and held it in her

trembling hands. "I noticed that they have no eyes, and the smell is awful." She tiptoed over the creatures' bodies. "My lord they're disgusting."

"Come on, we don't have much time," Max said.

"Why did you cut their heads off?"

"Because I'm not a priest."

"I don't understand."

"Priests cast out demons. I cut their heads off."

Sara's heart pounded with fear and anticipation at every step. Now she knew what she was getting into.

They moved several corridors before stopping. "Do you hear that?" Max asked Sara.

Faint thumps trembled from a distance. "It seems to be coming from the end of the hallway."

The thumps became louder, maintaining themselves in sequence like a drum to a death march. "If anything resembles a demon, kill it," he said.

"Are you talking about the Noraphamara?"

"That's right."

The thumps became louder and then ended by fading in silence. Max approached the door with his weapon still at the ready position. The door ticked and scraped from friction, yet did not open. He tapped the barrel of his .45 on the disabled steel door. "Room service." He then quickly examined the door for any signs of damage.

"That's not funny, Max."

The thumps resumed, but not from the steel door. This time they were louder and deeper than before. Sara looked over to her right. "Look, another staircase, and it sounds like the drum beat is coming from upstairs," she said. The darkness filled the length of the staircase, causing the unknown thump to haunt Sara's imagination. She followed Max up the stairs knowing that the unfortunate possibility of another attack could be at hand. *I cannot, and will not, chicken out now,* she thought. *I must keep going, for my father.*

"Stay close," Max said. "No matter what."

"Absolutely!" Sara's finger tapped nervously at the trigger. "Can you see?" her voice slightly trembled.

"I can see just fine," he said.

"I can't see a thing."

"My helmet activates its infra-red system when sensing darkness."

Sara turned to see if the lights from the hallway were still there, but she and Max were too far up the staircase. Only a faint shadow of light remained. She turned back towards Max and held the sheath to his sword snug in her hand. "A helmet with intelligence. How convenient," she chuckled.

Max said nothing.

"I don't need a helmet to sense the darkness."

Max said nothing.

The thumping continued.

-3-

The steel door to the lab weakened from each violent attack that came in contact with its surface, but now the thumps became random and offbeat, no longer in sequence. Multiple roars and howls erupted into an evil chorus with each enforced strike.

"I don't think the table's going to hold them," Dr. Lizzie Dawson said.

"We don't have much time," Dr. John Smithers said.

Two other science officers, Dr. Jon Yumzickee, and Dr. Jan Boomen rushed to the Eclipse prototype and covered it with a silver tarp. Boomen pushed a button on the control panel that was at the far side of the lab. "Watch yourself, Yumzickee," she warned.

The prototype sunk into the floor by a hydraulic device that was attached to a small section of the lab, and a replacing floor panel covered the deep opening.

"It should be safe for the time being," Yumzickee said.

Kristoff Von-Stien rushed to one of the lab tables with the Eclipse blueprints and micro-chip samples that were placed in a case. "I have them all, Si-Liss," he said in a thick German accent.

The thumps echoed throughout the lab. THUMP! THUMP! THUMP! And the steel door weakened even more.

Von-Stien, Si-Liss, and the other physicists ran to the main lab office that was surrounded by thick clear metal walls and a door. Yumzickee tripped and fell to his knees.

"Jon!" Boomen shouted.

The others made it to safety.

The brutally beaten lab door ripped open like an aluminum can and six rabid Noraphamara rushed in. The first Noraphamara ripped the table that blocked the door in half with its claws, and then threw the two pieces aside.

"CLOSE THE DOOR, NOW!" Smithers shouted in fear.

"But, what about Jon?" Boomen said.

"It's too late. We must save ourselves. Kristoff, close the door!" Smithers demanded.

Von-Stien promptly activated the safety lock. Just before the clear door shut, one of the Noraphamara slipped its blood-stained claw through the opening. The door severed the Noraphamara's hand at the wrist and the beast squealed like a pig as its blood poured from the amputation.

"Oh, dear God in heaven," Dawson grimaced with her hand over her mouth.

"Si-Liss, give me the fire extinguisher from the wall," Von-Stien said.

The Manduurin quickly grabbed the extinguisher and tossed it to Von-Stien. "What are you going to do?" he asked.

"Cover your eyes," Von-Stien said just before he slammed the butt of the extinguisher at the control panel to the door. Sparks from the door flew everywhere, and the lights flickered when it malfunctioned from the impact.

Yumzikee screamed in terror as two Noraphamara grabbed him by his arms and legs, both creatures at opposite sides. They pulled him violently. It was like a game to them, a game of tug-of-war that children play. His screams became louder from the pain.

"Oh my God, Jon!" Boomen cried as he heard the sounds of muscles tearing, and bones cracking from the stress of separation.

Yumzikee's body ripped in half, but his small intestine and large intestine were still intact. Blood and other loose organs poured out and splashed onto the floor. The two demonic beasts trembled in pleasure and lust for their unspeakable black craft. One of the two Noraphamara picked up Yumzikee's liver and shoved the organ into its mouth. Smithers vomited. "Forgive me guys," he said, gasping for breath.

The amputee Noraphamara slammed its bloody stump against the door and it roared in hunger, "KOOKKA MIIM!"

"How did the Noraphamara breach our security?" Von-Stien questioned.

"The question is, how'd they reach Earth? How did they find us?" Si-Liss said.

"I hope the door holds them," Dawson said.

"If not, as you humans would say in a time like this, 'You can kiss our ass's good-bye," Si-Liss said. "Wait, I forgot." The Manduurin grabbed a blaster from the desk cabinet. "Now we have a fighting chance."

"This doesn't make any sense, Si-Liss. Your people told us that the Demonixa didn't know where your race had migrated," Dawson said.

Si-Liss looked at Dawson with puzzlement. "I don't have all the answers, Lizzie, and I don't know how, or why, the Noraphamara are here."

The Noraphamara continued to eat Yumzikee's intestines, but the doctor's life did not cease. He looked up at Boomen and watched her in tears as he cried to death from the pain of being ripped apart and eaten alive.

The two Noraphamara managed to fully separate Yumzikee's carcass and then played with the remains. The other three Noraphamara ransacked the lab, looking for any pieces of the Eclipse. They threw chairs, tables, and smashed glass beakers filled with liquid at the wall. All six Noraphamara howled in a black mass chorus, like vamped wolves worshiping the full moon.

Two shots were fired and the demon with the stubbed arm fell lifeless from two large bullet holes: one in its back that exited out through its stomach, and the other at the back of the head; its brains vacuumed out into the open. Blood smeared on the door from the Noraphamara's claw, which followed the body down to the floor. The five remaining Noraphamara ceased their feeding frenzy and jerked their heads toward the unexpected shots.

"BEEAAX!" a Noraphamara hissed.

"That's right, kiddies," Max said while holstering his weapon.

The demonic creatures briefly paused in silence.

"What, no comment from the peanut gallery?" He unsheathed his sword and twirled it to where the flat edge of the blade was resting on his shoulder.

Sara looked around the edge of the door to the lab entrance. Max stood silent and waited patiently for the beasts to attack.

"VIISST VXX!" one beast hissed.

The two Noraphamara closest to Max attacked quickly and ramped; their movements looked deformed and unorthodox.

Max led the counterstrike by moving to the side, dropping to one knee, and simultaneously severing the leading Noraphamara's lower legs off. The beast came to a dead stop. Max then thrust up into the air and into a 360-degree spin. The momentum of the spin helped him attack quickly and powerfully, while diagonally slicing downward at the second Noraphamara's torso, causing it to split in two. However, the base of the body was still connected at the waist.

Sara gathered enough guts to finish the attack. "Max, I've got the blasted thing!" she shouted.

Max rolled to the side and out of the way of Sara's aim. Sara then fired at the split torso. The Noraphamara splattered onto the floor; its remaining body parts twitched on the ground like a dying insect.

Sara's heart pounded so hard she thought it would explode. "Max, to your right!"

Max turned, but it was too late. Two Noraphamara tackled him to the wall. He dropped his sword and gasped for air. The other remaining Noraphamara hissed at Sara and then rushed towards her. She raised her shaky arms and managed to fire directly at the attacking beast's cranium. Its partially headless body fell limp to the floor onto its own feces.

Max slipped his way out from the Noraphamara's grasps. "Sara, get out of the way!" he shouted.

The two Noraphamara ignored Sara and continued with Max. He quickly raised his fists.

The two beasts roared and swung their claws at him. Max tucked, parried and landed a side kick to one of the beast's knee caps, then quickly snapped its neck and kicked its lifeless body down. With an immediate movement, he trapped the last Noraphamara's arm and snapped its elbow with his forearm. He then ended the attack with a palm heel strike to the beast's nose, driving its cartilage into its brain. The body fell like a brick. "I win," he said.

Max looked at Sara

Sara relaxed the .12 gauge in her arms. "You're nuts."

Max's helmet covered his crooked smile. "That was a kick in the pants, wasn't it?" He picked up his sword. "At least I didn't cut off their heads," he said while sheathing his weapon.

"You're getting more civilized by the minute," she remarked with a smile.

The physicists thumped their fists to get Max's attention.

"Get us the hell out of here," Von-Stien's voice muffled.

"The door must be stuck," Sara said.

Max tapped on the door. "Clear metal," he murmured. He then placed his wrist blaster at the door to scan its texture and thickness. After the scanning process was finished, Max stepped away from the door and aimed the liquid weapon. "Move away from the door." He fired and the blast separated the door's molecular density no more than a fraction of a second, and formed the door into a brittle block of ice. Max unsheathed his sword, rammed it into the block of ice, and the top half crumbled down.

Sara stared at the shredded lab door to make sure that there were no surprises. "Do you think we've seen the last of those God-forsaken creatures?"

"They're like a bad rash."

"And?" she asked.

"That's it."

"Okay, I'll take that as a no," Sara replied.

Si-Liss was the last to come out from the room. He noticed the Corps symbols on Max's gloves. "You're one of us," he said.

"You could say that," Max nodded. "And who are you?"

"I am Dr. Si-Liss," he said, "and this is Dr. Kristoff Von-Stien."

Max turned to the other physicists. "And you two must..."

"Max," Sara interrupted, "my father isn't here." Her voice trembled.

Max looked at Sara. "This day keeps getting better."

Sara took off her hood. "Do you know where my father is, Doctor?" Sara asked.

"Yes, yes I do," Si-Liss said. "Dr Tontoo-K and Dr. Manning were sent to Mars…"

"I'm sorry, what did you say?" Max said. "What the hell are they doing there?"

"So my father is okay?"

"Well, I think so. Why?" Si-Liss said.

"Where on Mars?" Max asked.

Von-Stien pulled out a pack of cigarettes from the inside of his lab coat. "Near the Eve colony." He lit the cigarette with shaky hands, and inhaled deeply. "At the Pyramids of Cydonia." Then he exhaled.

Max sheathed his sword. "And the Eclipse prototype?"

"The prototype is here with us, but Manning and K have the activation chips," Si-Liss said. "They're still working out the glitches."

"By the way, what are the Noraphamara doing here?" Dr. Smithers asked.

"The Noraphamara have been sent to kill the four physicists who duplicated the Eclipse and destroy the prototype," Max said to Von-Stien and Si-Liss. "Consider yourselves famous, boys. You four have just made it to Carnmassicre's top five shit list."

"Who's the fifth on the list?" Boomen asked.

"Yours truly, Sister. You could say that I'm a little thorn in his back that can't be reached."

"There must have been a leak, or a spy," Si-Liss said. "But I don't understand how or why, I mean Carnmassicre was..."

"Look, Doc, it's not rocket science to know why the enemy wants you dead, just be happy that you're alive and kicking. I'm sorry to end the tea time chat, but I don't have much time to spare, so here's what I want you to do. I want you to contact the council and let them know what's going on and the problem will be taken care of. Can you do that for me? Can I count on ya, Doc?"

"Y-yes, yes we'll do that," Si-Liss said.

"And Doc, it would be a good idea to keep that blaster at hand till soldiers arrive," Max said. He lured Sara aside. "I need you to stay here with the physicists. You'll be safe here with them."

Sara shook her head. "No, I can't just stay here and wonder if my father's alive or not."

Max headed for the lab door. "I don't think so, girlie. You're staying here."

Sara grabbed Max's arm firmly. "Max, I need to know for myself. This will sound stupid, but he's the only father I have."

Max buckled his lips together in frustration. *Dammit,* he thought. Max knew that there were going to be problems ahead with the other two physicists on Mars. *Mars for God's sake, and of all the physicists, the girl's father had to be the one who had to get stationed on Mars. Dammit, why can't life be somewhat easy?* "Fine, just remember the rule."

"Thank you, Max," Sara said.

Max nodded. *Thanks... I just hope I don't get the girl killed.*

-4-

In the voids of the Delta-1 system, approximately 52,000 km to the Martian moons, a mid-sized starship called *The Noxious* thrust its way through space, with what sounded like a smooth, deep, humming whistle coming from the engine's core.

Inside the bridge of the ship, Minda sat patiently in her chair. Three of her conjured demons sat in suspended seats in front of a computer panel with their claws hovering over red circular beam sensors that controlled the ship. A Noraphamara with peach flesh entered the bridge and knelt like a loyal dog beside Minda's feet. "Ah, my child, my dearest pestilent," she soothed softly as if she were its mother.

"NOOMMAASSTTA," the Noraphamara wheezed deeply.

Minda leaned forward. "Soon, my child... soon," she said while softly stroking its eyeless face.

"WEELLFFAASST FAATTHHIISSTTA," it wheezed back.

Minda stood up with a haunting grace from her chair. The Noraphamara bowed its head like a servant and slithered its bulky body back from her feet. Minda looked at the stars through the visual screen with her arms folded, her hands caressing her own shoulders in perverse thought. *The lamb frolics amongst the land, and its shepherd stands before it with spoiled bread and infected wine.*

The Noraphamara rose from the floor and then walked with a slouch towards Minda, its pointed tongue licking the tips of its teeth. "FEESST FEECCIIT," the creature hissed.

Minda turned to the Noraphamara and noticed the creature's hunger, but she didn't say a word, just a soft *Mmmmmmmmmm,* as an alluring thought crossed her perverted mind. It was perhaps the thought of what the Noraphamara had just said; the thought of bathing in shepherd's blood. Minda returned to the visual scene. "There," she pointed out, "the land Cydonia." She moved to her chair and leaned back with her legs crossed. Her sapphire eyes glistened as the lids squinted to a sharp slant.

"LUUFFTTNNA?" one of the piloting Noraphamara asked.

"Yes, resume course and be aware," she said. "They might be watching."

Minutes later, the Noxious entered the Martian atmosphere. The ship landed near the mysterious face that was a few miles away from the Cydonian pyramids. The twin moons hung dim over the red surface.

Half a mile away, a land rover occupied with three soldiers was making a routine survey of the area and spotted the alien spacecraft. The rover stopped abruptly.

"Lieutenant, you see that?" Corporal Kiltin pointed.

"Affirmative, Corporal," Second Lieutenant Kimble said.

"That doesn't look like any of ours," PFC. Stratin said.

Struthers pushed a button to the com-link that was located at the side of his helmet. "General, over."

Brief static.

"Report, over," Brigadier General Martin responded.

Brief static.

"Sir, is there a ship scheduled to land, over?"

Brief static.

"Negative, Lieutenant, over?"

Static.

Kimble looked over at Kiltin. "Then we have an unscheduled landing, sir, over."

Static, then a pause.

"What are you talking about, Lieutenant. We have no record of such a landing, over."

Stratin looked at Kimble and Kiltin. "That doesn't make any sense, sir," Stratin said.

Kiltin looked puzzled.

"Nothing appeared on the scanner? Over," Kimble asked.

Static.

"Did the Manduurins come up with a new fighter, you think?" Stratin queried.

"I have my doubts," Kiltin said.

"Negative..." *Static*. "…where did the ship land, over?"

Static.

"At the north-west side of the Cydonian face, over."

Static.

"What's your twenty, over?"

Brief static.

"South-east end of the face, sir, over."

Static interference chopped Martin's transmission.

"What did he say?" Kimble asked the others. "Repeat, sir, you're chopping, over."

The transmission returned clear. "Check sight and report back, over."

Slight static.

"Yes, sir, out," Kimble ended.

They jerked back when Stratin buried the fuel peddle to the floor. The sandy surface flipped in a dust pattern from the wheel spin.

Kiltin monitored their weapon status. "Weapons at full charge, sir," he said.

"If anything should happen, CYA, boys," Kimble said.

"CYA, sir?" Stratin asked.

"That's right, Private," Kimble returned.

"Cover-your-ass," Kiltin said.

"Keep that in mind and you'll do fine, soldier."

"Yes, sir," Stratin replied.

Minutes later they arrived at the sight. Stratin eased his foot off the fuel pedal and the land rover slowed to a stop. They exited out from the rover with their rifle blasters at hand.

"Sir, we're on sight, over," Kimble said.

Static filled the com-link and then dissipated to a clear transmission.

"What's the ship look like, over?" Martin came back.

The three soldiers tucked themselves on a small hill with only their heads and blasters peaking over.

"I don't have a clear sight, sir, but all I can tell you is that it's a mid-size vessel and has florescent red trim, over," Kimble said.

Kiltin looked through his rifle scope and twisted the dials at the base of it. "The infra-red is activated, sir," he said.

"What's it look like?" Kimble asked.

"Well, sir, I don't think it's ours. I think it's Demonixian."

"Are you sure?" Kimble asked. "General, we think it's Demonixian, over."

Slight static.

"We really don't know much about the Demonixa; only what the Manduurin have told us..."

Stratin looked at Kiltin. "What about Tontoo-K? He's a Manduurin. He can tell us more about the Demonixa."

"So, if it is a Demonixian ship, wait for reinforcements then proceed with caution, over."

"Yes, sir, out," Kimble ended.

Kiltin twisted the long-range gauge on his scope. "That ship doesn't look like any of ours," he said, and then turned to Kimble. "It has to be a Demonixa; it has to be. It looks too freaky to be ours." He returned to the scope.

"How did the Demonixa reach the Milky Way? I thought..."

"You have to remember that the Demonixa can Event Horizon," Kimble said.

"Wait, Lieutenant. I see something coming out of the ship." Kiltin adjusted his position.

"Identify, Corporal," Kimble said.

Stratin squinted his eyes. "What is it?"

"Sir, it's a Noraphamara." Kiltin looked away from the scope and at Kimble.

"Are you sure?"

"Yes, sir. It is bulky, and slouched. Here look." Kiltin handed the rifle to Kimble.

Kimble lifted the rifle to position. "This isn't good." He handed the rifle back to Kiltin. "General, over."

The static became thicker.

"Re-ort, ov..."

"We have Noraphamara in sight, over."

"Wh-t's it d-ng?"

"Sir, I think the Noraphamara is carrying, wait, it is… it's a body," Kiltin said.

More static.

"General, the Noraphamara is carrying a body out of the ship."

"I think it's human, Lieutenant," Kiltin returned.

"And we think its human, over."

"Wait, sir..." Kiltin turned to Kimble. "The Noraphamara disappeared."

"Re-fo-cements are on th-..." Martin's transmission ended in thick static.

"This isn't a good sign," Stratin said.

"General, repeat, over," Kimble said.

Thick static.

"General, come in, over."

Thick static.

"General, over." Kimble lifted his weapon to position. "Fuck. Shit's gonna hit the fan with a splash, so watch your ass."

Like a silent, slow motion movie, two Noraphamara emerged from the Martian surface, awakened by an unnatural force. In seconds, the two creatures wheezed deeply.

The soldiers turned quickly toward the unknown wheezes. One of the Noraphamara licked its jagged teeth and the other hissed the words, "ZEEZ TOONNU!"

"Oh, shit!" Stratin shouted.

Kimble, Kiltin, and Stratin drew their blasters, but the Noraphamara retaliated by slapping the soldier's weapons aside with two powerful swoops. Struthers unsheathed his boot knife, then rammed and twisted the blade into one of the Noraphamara's abdomens. It screeched in pain, but didn't stop its attack.

Stratin was less fortunate. The other Noraphamara grabbed him by the neck and thrust its claw into the soldier's visor. The face shield exploded into fragments from the impact, causing his air supply to burst out into the Martian atmosphere. The creature's claw swallowed his face with its palm. The soldier choked and gasped for oxygen. The Noraphamara squeezed Stratin's skull until it caved in like a ripe pumpkin and then tossed the lifeless corpse to the side near a rock.

Kiltin pick up his blaster and violently slammed the butt end into the injured Noraphamara's skull. "Take that, you son-of-a-bitch!" he grunted.

The creature jerked back to gather its balance, then growled at Kiltin. Kiltin's heart pounded and his hands shook, yet he swallowed the fear and clenched his teeth. "Come and get it, ya bastard." He aimed the blaster at the Noraphamara's chest and fired. The Noraphamara cried in a squeal as its chest became a large hole. The creature fell to its knees while sticking its claws into the deep wound.

Kiltin quickly turned to the other Noraphamara, but Kimble was already on top of the creature with the tip of his knife aimed at the beast's head.

"Lieutenant, get out of the way! I don't have a clear shot!" Kiltin shouted.

In an adroit movement, Minda sliced Kiltin's head clean off. His hands released the blaster with a twitch and the body fell dead. Kimble looked up at Minda with a blank gaze, like he was hypnotized.

"Where is your shepherd now?" Minda said.

Tears fell from Kimble's eyes.

Minda placed her double-edged blade at Kimble's air support line. "Now I lay you down to sleep..." She then cut through the line. "…pray of me, and your soul I will keep," she whispered in blasphemy.

Kimble tried to grab the severed support line. He tilted off the Noraphamara, and gasped and wheezed for dear life.

The minion looked down at Kimble, her eyes clenched and her head slightly tilted back. "I forgive you, my child," she whispered in a chuckle, and watched in patience as the last remaining soldier faded away.

Minda then turned to the Noraphamara. "There are two other physicists on this world. Vanquish anyone who stands in your way," she commanded. "Now go."

"SUUBBLLIIS!" the Noraphamara bellowed, then withered into dirt and disappeared into the planet's surface.

–5–

Static filled the com-link speaker that was located above the communication computer panel.

Martin's eyes gazed at the speaker. "Lieutenant, over."

There was no response, just thick static.

"Lieutenant..."

"Sir," Lance Corporal Baker said. "Their vital signs have flat lined, sir."

"Christ!" Martin blurted. "And there's nothing showing on our long or short range sensors?"

Baker turned with his chair towards the general. "No, sir, the weather's clear. What do you think is out there, sir?"

A look of concern covered Martin's face. "I have no idea, Corporal." He walked to his desk and pulled out a field map of Cydonia from the upper right drawer. "I have a bad feeling about this," he said as he unfolded it on the desk. "Corporal, transmit a code red to the Eve colony and..."

"We have a breach in the main," a muddled voice said through the speaker. "...I repeat... in the main... entrance... th... I repeat... they're coming... the ground..."

Then the transmission ended in thick static.

"Transmit the distress call. Do it now, Corporal!" Martin ordered.

"Yes, sir."

Martin pulled out his side arm to check to see if the energizing crystal was up to level.

"Sir, our transmission isn't going through to Eve," Baker said.

Martin holstered the weapon. "Keep trying."

"Yes, sir."

The entrance door opened and seven soldiers walked in wearing dark blue BDUs and full battle gear. The soldiers saluted the general.

"Reporting, sir," First Lieutenant Gigglis said.

Martin returned the salute. "Then maybe you could tell me what the hell is going on down there, soldier."

"Sir, we have a Noraphamara infestation out there."

"Noraphamara, Lieutenant?"

"Sir," Baker interrupted, "my transmissions aren't getting through and all communications are out, perhaps temporarily."

Martin nodded.

"Yes, sir."

"Fuck," Martin murmured underneath his breath "Corporal, how long will it take you to reroute the transmitter system?"

"About an hour, sir," Baker said.

"Make it half, Corporal. Time is limited."

"Sir, right away."

"Now we know who is blocking our transmissions," Martin said.

"What makes Cydonia a prime target? I don't understand. I thought the Demonixa were still light years away from the Milky Way," Specialist Lipton said.

Martin reached into his coat breast pocket and pulled out a pack of Newports. "What makes us one of the prime targets?" He struck a match and lit the cigarette. "We have a lab with two of the four Eclipse physicists, so we have to watch their asses." He took a deep drag from the cigarette. "Corporal, add Earth to your transmissions list."

"Yes, sir."

Martin pinched the bridge of his nose with two fingers. "What do we know about the Noraphamara, First Sergeant?"

"The Noraphamara," First Sergeant Dunken said, " are a conjured Vok demon. In Manduurin translations, Norapha simply means *blind* and Mara means demon or more specifically, a demon who attempts to damn the soul. When conjured, their bodies become frail, yet slightly stronger than the average man. They're eyeless, so they have to rely on their sense of smell and hearing. They can be cannibalistic towards each other and if I remember right, the Noraphamara breeds beetle-like insects inside of its stomach called Innards. That's all I know, sir."

Martin took another puff from his cigarette. "The Noraphamara are still a mystery to us and the Manduurin."

"General, Major Monroe and the others have flat-lined," Baker informed.

Martin tossed the cigarette butt on the floor and smashed it with his boot. "What's the casualty count?"

Baker quickly typed. "Ten, sir."

Lipton took a long drink from his canteen. "Thank the Lord for water," he said after taking a breath with his head resting back on the wall.

"Our orders, sir?" Sergeant Major Siddy asked.

Martin picked up a map of Cydonia's inner structure. "Corporal, what was Major Monroe's twenty before flat line?"

"Between sections A and B, sir," Baker said.

"Alright." Martin displayed the map to the others. "I need you men to go directly to the main lab and bring Dr. Tontoo-K and Dr. Manning here. We need to make sure that they're okay and out of harms way. Is that understood?"

"Yes, sir," the soldiers said at once.

"Sir, what if the Noraphamara happen to find communications?" Siddy asked.

"Don't worry about that. The only concern you have is getting K and Manning here in one piece."

"Yes, sir."

"What about coms?" Gigglis asked.

Baker swiveled in his chair to face Gigglis. "I'm working on it now, Lieutenant," he said.

Martin pulled out another cigarette. "For the meantime we'll have com silence until Baker or I transmit to you first."

The computer's warning system activated.

The general turned to Baker. "Corporal, report."

"Sir, it appears to be coming from the sixth level..." Baker turned to the general, "...in the main system's support room."

"Life support status," Martin said.

Baker returned to the computer screen. "Fine for the moment, sir."

"They're trying to cripple us," Sergeant Bloomer said.

"Maybe," said Dunken.

Martin took two deep drags from his cigarette, inhaled deeply and smashed the butt on the floor. "Change of plans, men," he said. "Lieutenant..." Gigglis had strait eye contact with Martin. "...I need you and Lipton to go to systems support and check the disturbance. We should have coms on line soon."

"Understood, sir," Gigglis said.

The two soldiers walked out of the room.

"Watch your ass out there, men," Martin said. He then turned to the others. "And I need you men to go to level five and bring the physicists here. Hopefully the enemy hasn't found what they are looking for. When you engage the enemy, confront with extreme prejudice."

"Sir," the soldiers said and saluted.

Gigglis and Lipton entered the sixth floor main corridor. The torchlight flickered in a dance off the walls in sequences with their fire-tipped bases. The two soldiers held their rifle blasters ready with their index fingers at the trigger.

"Lieutenant, look," Lipton whispered. "Two torches are missing."

"Keep your eyes pealed, Lipton."

They continued onward towards the main system's support room that was at the end of the corridor. When they arrived at the room's entrance, they discovered a clear-based residue at the tips of the shredded door.

"What in God's name?" Lipton murmured.

Gigglis peaked in through the forced entrance with his blaster pointed upright. The room seemed to be untouched, yet he was puzzled as to why the door was the only thing vandalized and two torches were missing from the wall.

"Any thoughts, Lieutenant?" Lipton asked.

"Wild goose chase… ring a..." a muddled voice said through the soldier's com ear piece. "...tenant... do... copy, over?"

"I repeat. Lieutenant, report status, over," Martin returned, with a clearer reception.

"Sir, I see that we've resumed communications, over," Gigglis said.

"For the meantime, Lieutenant, all in-house coms are on line, but long-rang coms are still off line." Martin's voice slightly wavered, yet it was understandable. "Report status, over."

Gigglis pressed his earpiece. "Our breach was a hoax, sir. Only the entrance was badly damaged, over."

A pause and then static.

"Regroup with the others and..."

Martin's voice cut in and out of the static and was simultaneously replaced with another voice, which had a rapid and tense sound to it.

"What the hell was that?" Lipton asked.

"General, you're breaking up. Repeat orders, sir, over," Gigglis said.

The voice faintly returned.

Gigglis quickly turned to Lipton. "Can you make out the transmission?"

Lipton shook his head. "Not a clue, sir." The soldier briefly paused. "Wait..." He looked at the lieutenant.

The transmission cleared.

"It could be Sergeant Dunken," Lipton said.

"We've been ambushed... if anyone can hear me... need back-up, over," Dunken's voice soared.

Gigglis pressed the earpiece. "What's your twenty, Sergeant, over?"

Brief static.

"Level four, north end of the first corridor... I don't know how... long we can hold... over."

"Lipton and I are on our way. Hold tight, Sergeant, out," Gigglis ended.

The two soldiers engaged in a mad dash down the corridor with their hands gripped to their blasters and their hearts pounding with adrenaline. The smell of ozone filled the corridor and a cloud of smoke hovered over the freshly spilled blood area. With each Noraphamara that was dropped, another would take its place in battle by rising from the ground. Some would engage in cannibalistic behavior, while the others rushed in a bloodshed attack. Sweat dripped from the soldiers' faces, their eyes burned, and their teeth clenched from the pain of salt entering their corneas. Still their defenses were unbroken.

"We're surrounded!" Corporal Smitty shouted in a panic.

"Focus, soldier. Don't let it get to you," Siddy said.

"Shit, I'm out," Dunken shouted.

Bloomer pulled out an extra energizing crystal from his pouch and tossed it. "Sergeant," he said.

In a moment's time, the sandy surface became like soggy oatmeal, engraving their every step.

The corridor was overwhelmed by the pugnacious stench of decomposing Noraphamara skin, yet the remaining cannibalizing demons continued to binge on their dead. Two Noraphamara managed to break through the soldiers' defenses and brutally slammed Smitty and Bloomer to the ground. The two soldiers coughed while gasping for air.

"Major..." Smitty gasped.

Sergeant Major Siddy raised his blaster rifle and rammed the butt of it into the Noraphamara's back. The creature's teeth dripped as it growled at Siddy, yet the Noraphamara had no intention of releasing Smitty from its clutches.

"Do you want more, you son-of-a-bitch?" Siddy grunted. He thrust the butt of the blaster into the Noraphamara's mouth. Fragments of teeth spilled onto the sand, followed by blood dripping from its lacerated lips. Smitty pulled out his boot knife from its sheath and gathered enough strength to force the blade into the Noraphamara's neck. The creature fell limp with blood leaking from its clogged wound.

"Siddy, behind you!" Smitty warned.

Siddy looked over his shoulder as his eyes widened from the sight of jagged teeth dripping a clear discharge from the gums down to the lips.

"Sweet Jesus!" he said and raised his rifle.

-6-

The Eclipse mogul chip hung suspended by a blue beam of light in a 2" x 5" clear cylinder. The microchip rotated slowly while Dr. Seth Manning examined its crystal fibers. The fibers sparkled through the lens of the microscope as he stimulated the ignition compositor with a red beam. Tontoo-K placed a black briefcase with silver trim and a silver insignia of the Corps on the lid, on the lab table near Manning and the microscope. He then opened the case by pushing the insignia. Six of the same identical chips rested comfortably in separate sponge compartments.

"Thank you, K," Manning said.

The Manduurin nodded.

Manning adjusted his glasses. "The compositors are aligned perfectly, K. We'll have at least seven ready to go in no time at all," he said.

Tontoo-K rolled the blueprints and schematics to the Eclipse in brown cylinders, then leaned them on the wall.

"Finished," Manning said as he inserted the last chip into the sponge compartment. "The chips are ready for trans..."

Suddenly the lab door trembled with a muffled thump, like someone was slamming a large rubber mallet against the surface, followed by loud wicked howling.

The physicists quickly looked up.

"What in God's name?" blurted Dr. Manning.

"By the moons of Tyruss, it's Noraphamara," Tontoo-K said.

"Are you sure, K?"

"How could I forget? My people succumbed to the hands of Noraphamara," Tontoo-K said in discomfort.

Another great thump from the door.

Manning ran to the lab-com. "General, we have a breach in the main lab. I repeat..."

"Manning, there's no time. We have to escape."

"BLAST IT!" Manning spat in a Scottish accent. "Grab the blueprints and schematics." Manning picked up the black briefcase from the table and ran. He opened a hidden door that was at the back wall of the lab. They quickly entered the passageway and closed the door behind them, or so they thought.

The main entrance gave way and a group of Noraphamara spilled into the lab like mad dogs; seconds later Minda followed. Her eyes squinted as she surveyed the room. The Noraphamara stood anxious near Minda's side with their nostrils flared from the scent of the two physicists.

Minda walked over to the open safe and grazed her fingers at the edge of the opening. "I want them found," she said. "Bring them to me alive or in pieces."

"MIIS PLLIIPPTTOON," a Noraphamara said.

Sara grimaced at the sight of two slaughtered bodies

which lay scattered in their unfortunate positions. She tried to keep her emotions from erupting, not to mention her queasy stomach. "I think I'm going to be sick," she said.

"Keep yourself together, Sara."

Max noticed movements from a distance. He holstered his weapon and promptly approached the object. When he arrived, the light from the burning torches revealed a severely butchered soldier with two stubbed legs. The soldier's head swayed slowly with his bloody stubs dragging and creating an armless snow angel in the sand. His arms were nowhere to be found.

Max knelt beside the soldier.

"I've seen the devil..." the soldier whispered.

"What did he say?" Sara asked.

"Where did you see the devil?" Max asked.

"I see so much clearer now..." the soldier continued. "I see so much..."

"Did they take the physicists?" Max asked.

"I don't kn-know, sir..." With a hard choke, blood filled his mouth and dribbled onto his cheek. "I can't feel my arms or my legs, sir. Wh-what happened to them?" the soldier faded.

Max shook the soldier lightly. "Stay with me, son," he said. "Tell me what happened to the physicists? Did you see them? Did someone take them?" Max knew deep down that the soldier wasn't capable of coherent answers.

"I can't feel my..." Choke! "The devil took my... legs." Then the soldier died.

Max closed the soldier's eyes. "I'll take his," he whispered.

"Max, is my father…?" Sara asked in a trembling voice.

Max looked up at her. "There's no reason to grieve yet."

Manning smacked his flashlight in frustration, while both he and Tontoo-K stood in complete darkness.

"Damn flashlight!" Dr. Manning cursed.

"Is the flashlight energized?" Tontoo-K asked.

"Yes. Blasted flashlight won't..."

With one last hard strike, the flashlight flickered to its full potential.

Manning smirked. "See, K. With a little finesse and sweet talk."

Tontoo-K shook his head. "I see," he said.

Manning pointed the flashlight towards the darkness, revealing a long continuous hallway that tied into the distant shadows. The physicists began to walk, gradually accelerating their stride.

"K, any ideas as to where this leads?"

"No, but I'm assuming that it leads us to the end of the hallway," he said.

"Funny, K. And I suppose that there's a leprechaun waiting for us at the end of the yellow brick road, willing to give us magical charms, right?"

"Don't be silly. We're not that lucky, Doctor. I've studied the structural blueprints, but I must have missed a few minor details," Tontoo-K said.

Manning shook his head and chuckled to himself.

When the two physicists came closer to the end of the hallway, the shadows blanketed them with a feeling of insecurity.

Manning adjusted his glasses by sliding his finger up the bridge of his nose. “I think I see something,” he said.

“Is it a way out?”

Manning turned to Tontoo-K. “I don’t know, maybe.”

“Maybe, you say?”

When they reached the end of the hallway, three separate stairwells became visible in the light, like doors in a game show. The two physicists looked at each other with dismay.

“Any ideas?”

“It seems to me that this is just another of life’s disappointing choices.”

“Well, laddie, is it door number one, two, or three?”

“Shhhhh, listen. Do you hear that?” Tontoo-K crouched.

Manning briefly paused. “What is it?”

“You don’t hear that?”

“No. Me hearing isn’t as…” Manning paused again. “Shit. It’s them, isn’t it?”

Howling voices echoed faintly.

“We don’t have much time, so choose, Doctor,” Tontoo-K said.

“Blast, I can’t make up me mind, K,” Manning said in frustration.

The voices were no longer faint, but an echo; a loud echo.

“Do I have to choose for you, Manning?”

“Door number two,” Manning decided.

They quickly entered into the middle stairwell. It

was dark. The flashlight flickered.

"Blast." Manning gave the flashlight a hard strike. "Sometimes we don't have that luxury, K," he said.

In the communication's room.

Martin waited while Baker scanned the computer database for several encrypted codes to transmit a distress call to the Eve colony.

Minutes later.

"No luck, sir," Baker said.

Martin gave a look of frustration. "Keep trying, Corporal," he said.

"Yes, sir."

The door opened. Siddy, Bloomer, and Dunken entered the room in a mess. Blemishes of human and Noraphamara blood mixed together like a bad Pollack painting on their torn BDUs. The soldiers were tired, but they remained focused. Dunken sighed while wiping the sweat from his forehead.

"Reporting, sir," Siddy said, catching his breath.

"What happened to the others?" Martin asked.

Bloomer took a long drink from his canteen and then poured some onto his face.

"Flat lined, sir," Siddy said.

Martin turned to Baker. "Are vital signs functioning properly, Corporal?" he asked.

"Yes, sir. But..." Baker turned to Martin, "…my sensors indicate all life signs are fine, sir."

"Dammit," Martin cursed. "Sir, we lost communications, but I managed to contact Gigglis as we were engaging the Noraphamara."

"General," Baker called, "I hear a faint transmission

on line." Baker managed to clear up the jumbled voice.

"Assistance, over," Gigglis's voice cut in.

"Repeat transmission, over," Martin said.

"The lab's been ransacked... no sign... Manning nor Dr. Tontoo... need assistance for clean sweep of the area, over," Gigglis said.

"Are you in the main lab now, Lieutenant, over?"

"Yes, sir, over."

"Stay at your twenty. Siddy, Bloomer, and Dunken will meet you there, over."

"Understood, sir, out."

Baker handed Martin three other com-links from the console drawer. "These should maintain transmissions," Baker said.

"Are the com-links in code?" Martin asked.

"Yes, sir," Baker said.

"Will Gigglis and Lipton be able to transmit with the other coms?"

"Yes, sir. I created a code that will be compatible. They should work."

Martin traded com-links with Siddy and the others.

"Report as soon as you reach Gigglis's twenty," Martin ordered.

"Understood, sir," Siddy complied.

The soldiers walked out of the room.

Martin pulled out another cigarette and lit it. "Any luck, Corporal?" he exhaled.

"Negative, sir."

Martin dabbed the sweat from his forehead with the back of his hand. He puffed deeply and held the smoke in his lungs while engaged in thought. He rubbed his eyes and exhaled.

-7-

Tontoo-K looked over his shoulder, but there was nothing there, only darkness. *That's strange,* he thought. *I haven't heard a howl or a screech for a couple of minutes.*

"I see light, K," Manning announced.

Tontoo-K returned to Manning.

"It's faint, but it's light," Manning said.

"It's about time. This stairwell gives me the creeps," Tontoo-K said.

The faint torchlight flickered in a pattern and became brighter as they came closer to the end.

"We're almost there, K."

The flashlight dimmed to a weakening flicker.

"The dammed thing died," Manning said.

"We'll use the torchlight to guide us," K said.

When they finally reached the end, they discovered another hallway lit by torches.

"Grab a torch, Doctor," Tontoo-K said.

Manning dropped his flashlight into his lab coat and pulled a torch from the wall.

"Look for any openings, doors, or anything that will get us out of this mess," Manning said.

Tontoo-K looked over his shoulder. "So far, so good," he said.

"Just keep your round eyes pealed, K."

The physicists picked up their pace to a fast walk.

"I feel like a mouse in a maze looking for a piece of cheese," Manning said.

"I don't see any blood or body parts. That's a good sign," Gigglis said.

"Lieutenant," Lipton called.

"Did you find something?"

Lipton opened the escape door. "They must have cleared out before the Noraphamara could reach them," he assumed.

Gigglis pulled out his mini-flashlight from his right breast pocket. He aimed it into the dark passageway. "Well, I hope they made it safely," he said.

Slight static.

"Lieutenant, over," Struther's voice transmitted.

"Gigglis here, over," he said.

"Are you still at your twenty, sir?"

"Yes, over."

"We'll be there in ten, over."

"Copy that, Lieutenant, out." Gigglis stood up and walked to a lab table that was folded in half. Gigglis pushed on his ear piece. "General, over."

Static.

"Report, Lieutenant, over," Martin returned.

"General, the physicists have escaped, over."

"Are you sure, Lieutenant, over?"

"We assumed, sir." Gigglis walked to the opened safe that was at the wall. "There's no traces of blood and the safe is wide open, over."

Static.

"I don't like assumptions, Lieutenant. I need to know if Dr. Manning and Dr. Tontoo-K are alright, over."

"Yes, sir."

"Sir, there's scuff marks," Lipton said.

Gigglis nodded. "Yes, sir, understood, over."

Static.

"...out," Martin ended.

Lipton stood up. "Now what, sir?" he asked.

"We wait," Gigglis said.

Struthers, Bloomer, and Siddy ran through the hallway with their blaster rifles in hand, sweat dripping from their hair to their faces.

"Do you hear that?" Bloomer asked.

"Not a thing, Sergeant. Just keep running," Siddy said.

Suddenly, a gnarled hand shot up from the sand and clamped Siddy's ankle. Siddy fell to a dead stop in the sand. "Aaaaaaaaa!" he shouted. "Something's…"

Struthers and Bloomer stopped and looked back.

"What the fuck?" Bloomer blurted.

With one smooth motion, a Noraphamara rose from the sand with Siddy's ankle in hand. The beast howled as it lifted Siddy off the ground.

"Fuck!" Siddy shouted as he dropped his blaster rifle.

"HIIX LEEPPQ!" the creature hissed, as it raised its clawed hand.

"What's it doing?" Bloomer asked.

"I don't care what it's doing, shoot the fucker before

it rips me apart!" Siddy shouted.

Struthers and Bloomer aimed their blasters at the beast. Three other Noraphamara that rose behind the two soldiers added more howls to the first.

"Oh shit! Move!" Struthers shouted.

Struthers and Bloomer tucked and rolled from the Noraphamara's grasp. Struthers pulled out his boot knife and threw it at the head of the Noraphamara that had Siddy's ankle. The blade stuck deep into its cranium. The beast fell back as it dropped Siddy on his side. He landed with a thud, knocking the air out of his lungs. "God that hurt," he coughed.

"Look out Lieutenant!" Bloomer shouted as he shot multiple times at the Noraphamara's chest.

The beast squealed.

The other two Noraphamara rushed Struthers like rams, slamming him to the wall. Struthers coughed, wheezed, and gasped for air. One of the beasts slapped the lieutenant's blaster from his hand, then pinned him firmly to the wall.

"Get these mother fuckers off me!" he shouted.

Bloomer aimed his blaster at the Noraphamara.

"Don't shoot, Sergeant!" Siddy said.

"I have the bastards in my sights," Bloomer said.

"The lieutenant is too close," Siddy said.

"Fuck!" Bloomer yelled. He raised his blaster and crammed it into one of the Noraphamara's kidneys. The Noraphamara gasped in a painful wheeze.

"How'd that taste, Jack!" Bloomer grunted.

The Noraphamara limped slightly, but didn't fall. The beast turned around and backhanded Bloomer to the opposite wall, then lunged at him. Siddy pulled out his boot knife and stuck the double-edged weapon into the other Noraphamara's neck. The beast made a gurgling sound. Siddy pulled the blade from the beast's neck and then thrust it into its kidney. Thick black and yellow liquid dripped from the blade like multi-colored syrup as he pulled it from the beast's organ. The Noraphamara fell to its side with its bloody neck tilted and its head resting on the wall.

Bloomer struggled with the last remaining Noraphamara; its teeth dripped saliva as it chattered in hunger.

"Aaaaaaaaaaaaaaaaaaa! I'm pinned, get it off me!" Bloomer shouted.

Struthers and Siddy tackled the Noraphamara off of Bloomer's body.

"Man these fuckers are strong," Siddy said.

"Hold it!" Struthers grabbed his boot knife and crammed the blade as far as he could into the Noraphamara's head. "DIE, SON-OF-A-BITCH!" he shouted while twisting the blade.

"This is getting old," Struthers said.

"Man, what I wouldn't do for an ice cold beer and a rubdown right about now," Bloomer coughed.

"Our time is limited, men," Struthers said.

The soldiers picked up their gear and hightailed it down the hallway.

The sand rose from its surface, pulled by an invisible and inverted hourglass, forming a sculpture and changing color to a dark gray, and then in to a charcoal black. The creature squealed, then purred, and then howled, ending in what sounded like a whimper. The remaining grains of sand that kept their native color fell from the beast's shoulder like salt from a shaker. The conjured Noraphamara's teeth chattered in anticipation. Food was near.

Tontoo-K's eyes bugged when he heard the distant howl. "Did you hear that?" his voice slightly trembled.

"Yes I did, and it would be a good idea if we speed up our pace, don't you agree?"

Tontoo-K nodded.

"I wish I had me blaster about now," Manning said.

"Did you forget it in your quarters again?"

"Aye, I did. Can you believe it, K?"

"Do you want me to answer that, my earthling frien...?"

There was another deep howl, but closer than before.

"This isn't good, K."

"If we get out of this in one piece, I'm going to raise hell about the light situation in these hallways," Tontoo-K said.

Manning looked over his shoulder to K. "You do thaaaaaaaaaaaaaaaaa............"

"Aaaaaaaaaaaaaaaaaaaaaaaa!!!!!!!!!!!!!!" Tontoo-K shouted in surprise, as the two physicists fell into a shadowy void.

The torch slipped from Manning's hand. He watched the flickering stick drop until its glowing tip vanished.

Tontoo-K's eyes were wide open as he shouted at the top of his lungs all the way down the shadowy drop.

They landed hard with a muffling thud onto the sand. There was brief silence. Then a moan...

And a cough...

Then a groan...

And a gasp...

Manning turned his head and saw a distinct flame that was about an arm's length away from his body. "I… I have good news," he coughed. "And I have bad news."

Tontoo-K didn't move, and only breathed in a gasp. "Tell me the good news first, Manning," he groaned.

Manning took a deep breath. "The good news is, I found the torch."

"You didn't lose the briefcase, did you?" the Manduurin gasped.

"Aye."

"This isn't good."

"Do you have the blueprints and the schematics?"

"Well, yes and no."

The howl deepened and amplified.

"The Noraphamara is getting closer," Tontoo-K whispered.

Manning and Tontoo-K struggled to their hands and knees.

"I found the briefcase..." Manning groaned. "And my glasses."

"I hope it's..."

A thump and a whimpering squeal suffused the blackened room.

The two physicists paused.

"By the God in heaven," Tontoo-K whispered.

Manning pulled out his flashlight with a nervous hand. The bulb flickered twice before settling into a stable beam. Manning pointed at the sound and saw a

Noraphamara flicking its tongue.

"Oh shit. Now what, K?" Manning whispered.

"It's a black Noraphamara. We don't stand a chance."

"What do you mean, we don't stand a chance?"

"Just keep the light shined at the beast and start to walk back slowly," Tontoo-K whispered.

The Noraphamara's muscular torso expanded and contracted with each breath it took. Its eyeless face twitched as its nostrils inhaled the scent of the two physicists. It chattered its jagged teeth with its head tilted to the side.

The flashlight dimmed. "No, not now," Manning pleaded.

The black beast ceased its daunting chatter with a loud squeal. The flashlight dimmed to nothing. Manning tapped the head of the flashlight on his thigh. The bulb awakened for a second and then faded. The Noraphamara gave a loud and vicious roar in rabid lust for its prey.

At the same time, Manning yelled in war cry with his dimming flashlight raised high.

"What in God's name are you doing?"

The slouching Noraphamara rushed at the two physicists.

"Help, K!" Manning yelled.

Tontoo-K dropped the blueprints and schematics, then rushed into a dive towards the club that was once a torch.

Manning's hand clamped the briefcase handle like a vise as he counter rushed the Noraphamara with the flashlight.

The Noraphamara swung its right arm at Manning.

Manning tucked his head and retaliated by smashing the flashlight at the base of the creature's head. The upper part of the flashlight shattered. The forceful strike didn't really affect the Noraphamara, it only made it more angry.

"I just pissed the son-of-a-bitch off," Manning said.

Tontoo-K clubbed the Noraphamara's right kidney with all that he could muster. The beast gasped and torqued its back.

"DIE!" Tontoo-K shouted.

The Noraphamara swung its arm and struck Tontoo-K's chest, knocking him aside. Manning rushed at the black beast and stabbed its rib cage with the jagged end of the flashlight. "Die!" Manning shouted while thrusting the sharp object. "God-forsaken bastard!"

The Noraphamara shrieked while cupping its bloody wound with its right hand, while its left hand swooped at Manning's head. The physicist moved out of the way just before the Noraphamara made contact. Tontoo-K shook his head to gather his senses. The creature released its claw from its punctured wound and attacked Manning again. The Noraphamara's sharp nails shredded Manning's lab coat.

"Blast-it, K, help me!" Manning shouted.

The black beast hissed then shrieked at Tontoo-K, then at Manning.

"I can't see a thing; it's too dark in here," Tontoo-K said, as he picked up the club and held it firmly in his hands. "Wherever you are, duck!" He pulled his arms back to a batting position, and with one swift swing, the Manduurin bashed the Noraphamara in the head.

The sound of loud bones fracturing echoed in the darkness. The Noraphamara stumbled, but it managed to maintain balance. The wooden club almost split in two, but held together by a couple of strands of wood.

"Did I hit you?"

"No, I'm alright."

The beast roared.

Tontoo-K bent down to his hands and knees to find the blueprints and schematics. "Where are they?" he muttered and waved his hands in a circular pattern.

"Where are you, K?" Manning asked.

"I don't know where I am. How should I..."

The roar abruptly stopped.

"Shhhh... I think it's gone," Manning whispered

Tontoo-K stretched out his arm, his fingers bumped the schematics, or was it the blueprints? *Who knows; who cares,* he thought. He just knew that they were there within his grasp.

The beast chattered its teeth at the physicists even though it couldn't see them, and then whimpered in pain.

Tontoo-K crawled on.

Manning sat still in silence. He could hear the creature's movements. The physicist's hand sweated and began to cramp from clenching the briefcase handle, but that didn't matter; nor did the intense headache he was suffering from. His heart pounded, but he didn't move nor did he attempt to breathe.

Tontoo-K accidentally brushed the sand with his shoe. The Noraphamara ceased its whimpering. Tontoo-K didn't move or breathe. His arms shook and sweat dripped from his face. The Noraphamara returned with a hiss followed by heavy breathing. The breathing was more like sniffing. The creature was trying to locate the two physicists by their scent.

Tontoo-K, realizing that they were being stalked, felt his heart pound and began to shake. *Lying still isn't going to matter,* he thought

The Noraphamara squealed loudly, knowing that its prey was within reach.

It's too late! It's coming, it's coming, K thought while closed his eyes.

Yet before the Noraphamara could lunge at K, two shots were fired and the beast fell to the ground next to his feet.

"Having a bad day, Doc?" a voice followed.

– 8 –

Sara took off her helmet and embraced her father tightly. "I was so afraid that..."

"Sara?"

"I thought..."

"I'm fine, Sara, really I am," he said and smiled.

"Save the reunion for later," Max said.

"Now where are we?" Tontoo-K murmured. He looked at Max with his head slightly tilted. "By the way, who are you?"

"Just someone that was sent to help you," Max said.

"Look at his gloves, K," Manning said.

"I see."

"Who's the head cheese of this establishment?" Max asked.

"Brigadier General Martin," Tontoo-K said.

"And where is General Martin?"

"Communications," Manning said.

"Did you try..." Max paused and looked over his shoulder, and saw three sand hills forming from the surface.

"Max?" Sara said.

Max turned to the others. “Behind you!” he warned, as hills formed behind Sara and the physicists. “Stay close to your father.” He pulled out his .45s from their holsters and aimed them at the forming hills. Seconds later, six Noraphamara were born. They all screamed in a squeal that pierced Sara, Manning, and Tontoo-K’s ears. Max’s ears were sheltered from the vocal attack by his helmet. “This day isn’t going well at all,” Max said in frustration.

The three Noraphamara that were facing Max rushed at him. He fired without hesitation. One of the Noraphamara fell to the sand and landed face down. The other two were slightly wounded, but they kept charging towards Max. He continued to fire until the magazines were empty. The two beasts tackled Max. He dropped one of his .45s, slamming the other repeatedly at the base of one of the Noraphamara’s necks. Three other Noraphamara became flesh; two of the three were of the normal sandy brown color and the third was a charcoal black.

Tontoo-K’s eyes didn’t blink. “Shoot the black Mara first,” he said.

“Sara, give me the shotgun,” Manning said. He handed the briefcase to Sara. He cocked and aimed the rifle at the blackened beast and fired. In a quick movement, one of the brown Noraphamara jumped into the line of fire to protect its stronger counterpart. It held its ripped open abdomen with its hands as it fell to the side, dying before the black Noraphamara’s feet. The black beast squealed in hatred and in hunger. “LIIKKSSEEZ DUUPPRRU!”

“What did it say, K?” Manning asked.

"I don't know," Tontoo-K replied.

"What do you mean, you don't know? I thought your race knew all about the Noraphamara, especially their language."

"I don't, Doctor!" Tontoo-K said angrily.

"They're coming closer," Sara yelled and pointed at them.

Manning aimed the weapon again at the black Noraphamara. Tontoo-K turned to look back and noticed that Max was having trouble with two other Noraphamara. He handed Sara the blueprints and schematics. "Hold these for me, Ms. Manning." He then grabbed a torch from the wall and pulled back. "Excuse me."

The Noraphamara looked up at Tontoo-K with its mouth open and its tongue darting. The Manduurin yelled and swung the fire-tipped club at the beast with all he could muster. The thick part of the torch covered the creature's mouth on impact; its teeth shattered and its lower jaw dislocated, hanging like Jell-O. The beast fell back to the wall with its head lit up like a candle; its body torqued to one side, and its head pounced in a mad dance.

Max wrapped his arms around the other Noraphamara's neck and quickly applied pressure. The beast squirmed as its air supply was being cut off. "Goodnight," Max said in a groan, and the Noraphamara collapsed. Max pushed the beast off his legs. "Torch his ass before he wakes up, Doc."

Tontoo-K placed the flame on the Noraphamara's chest and watched its body burn. Another shotgun round was fired, another squeal was screamed, and another body had fallen. Only the black Noraphamara remained.

The beast roared deeply at Manning. "Is that right?" Manning squeezed the trigger, but there was nothing, just a click, a dry shot, and an empty chamber. He pulled two rounds from the stock ammo strap. The Noraphamara came closer to Manning. He walked backwards, but just before he could push the last round into the rifle, the blackened creature chattered its teeth and lunged at him.

"Sara, get out of the way!" Max shouted.

The Noraphamara slapped the shotgun out of Manning's hands as the weapon fired. It picked Manning up by his neck. Manning grabbed the creature's wrist as he gasped for air, but his hands were too weak.

Max and Tontoo-K made a mad dash for Manning. "VIIVVIIDDOODDA NORAPHAMARA!" the black beast summoned.

Before Max and Tontoo-K could reach Manning, two pairs of arms thrust up from the sand and tripped them both. Max looked over his shoulder and saw two Noraphamara bodies rising. Tontoo-K reached for the torch that he had dropped. "I can't reach it."

One of the Noraphamara picked up Tontoo-K by his neck and the other grabbed Max and slammed him to the wall, then threw him to the opposite wall. Tontoo-K gasped as his eyes rolled to their whites while his body dangled like a tea bag.

"Father!" Sara screamed.

Manning tried to kick the Noraphamara, but he was getting weak. "S-Sara... r-run," he choked.

Sara dropped the blueprints and schematics near the briefcase, then quickly picked up the shotgun and aimed it at the Noraphamara. "Let him go!" she said.

"Don't shoot!" Max shouted, seeing that her father was in the line of fire.

She turned to Max.

"Look out!" he shouted.

Before Sara could react, the Noraphamara struck her with the back of its hand and launched her to the wall. Even so, she managed to shoot the rifle, but the shot didn't kill the black beast, it only wounded it.

"VIIVVIIDDOODDA NORAPHAMARA!" it screeched.

Two other Noraphamara rose up from the sand.

Sara looked up at them with dazed eyes. "I can't... I..."

One of the Noraphamara squealed and the other picked Sara up by the hair. She screamed as she tried to resist.

"SIIDDOODDOO MINDA!" the black Noraphamara ordered.

The Noraphamara let go of Sara's hair and the other creature grabbed her by the arms and slung her over its muscular shoulder.

"Let me go!" Sara screamed.

"Let her go!" Manning grunted.

Max unsheathed his sword and lunged at the Noraphamara that had thrown him against the wall. The creature swung its arms at him like a bear. Max tucked and rolled out of the way of the attack, then retaliated by amputating the creature's legs at the kneecaps. The Noraphamara squealed when its bloody stubs hit the ground. Max ended the attack by decapitating the creature between its 3rd and 4th cervical vertebrae. Then, in an added fluent movement, Max pulled out a throwing dart filled with nerve agent from his left arm pouch and threw it at the Noraphamara that had Tontoo-K by the neck. The dart stuck in the beast's right thigh as it tilted its head back and roared. The Noraphamara pulled the dart from its leg. The dart's tip broke inside and the fatal liquid flowed. The beast let go of Tontoo-K seconds before its body succumbed to a deadly stagger.

"Wh-what was in that dart?" Tontoo-K coughed.

"Nerve agent, Doc. Nasty stuff."

The infected Noraphamara writhed. Thick mucus flowed from its nose and mouth, as it lost all bodily functions. The veins swelled under the skin, but didn't break through. It tilted its head back to the side, then side to back, then side-to-side. Then it bit its tongue, cutting it in two separate pieces. It then ripped its abdomen up to its chest wide open to release the pressure.

"SIIDDOODDOO MINDA, SIIDDOODDOO!" the black beast commanded. One of the Noraphamara pulled Sara from its shoulder and braced her in its thick muscular arms as she screamed in bloody terror.

"MAX!"

The creature covered her mouth with its hand and like quicksand, the surface swallowed Sara and the two Noraphamara. The terrified girl's screams were only harkened as muffled cries until the open mouth of the sand engulfed her. The black Noraphamara slammed Manning to the wall. Grains and chips of the wall's surface covered his shoulders and coat. His face turned to a light shade of blue as the creature squeezed tighter. Puffs of gasps were the only thing that escaped from his purple lips.

Max rushed at the black Noraphamara with his

sword clenched in his hand and raised. The black beast retaliated by throwing Manning at him and the two men collided like wrecking balls. Manning was knocked out cold from the impact. Max shook his head to gather himself.

Tontoo-K walked behind Max.

Max stood up, still slightly dazed. "Ouch!" he said with teeth clenched.

The Noraphamara attempted to lunge at Tontoo-K. Max stepped in front of the Noraphamara's attack and drove his sword as deep as he could inside of its abdomen. Tontoo-K quickly jumped out of the way.

Max and the Noraphamara hit the wall hard. He gathered enough strength to twist the sword in a half circle. Its blood leaked from the freshly opened wound, yet that didn't stop the Noraphamara from its attack. It then grabbed Max by his arms and slammed him at the wall. He coughed and grunted. Then the creature threw him at the opposite wall near Tontoo-K.

With a squeal of pain, the Noraphamara slowly pulled the sword from its body. Steady flowing multi-colored blood ran down its legs. It threw the sword aside and roared even louder than before.

"I have the son-of-a-bitch in my sights!" Smitty said.

The Noraphamara turned to the voice. Its teeth chattered and it let out a low roar. *An opening,* Max thought.

Before the Noraphamara could return its attention to Max, Max rushed at the beast and tackled it to the ground. "Take the physicists and get the hell out of here, now!" he shouted while struggling with the Noraphamara.

Siddy and Smitty rushed to help Manning from the ground and braced him with his arms resting on their shoulders. Tontoo-K quickly picked up the blueprints, schematics, and briefcase, and hightailed it to the other soldiers.

The Noraphamara tried to buck Max from its back, but Max retaliated by wrapping his arms around its neck for a choke hold. His arms acted as anacondas, with each resisting move the creature made, more pressure was applied to the choke. "Hugs," he said.

The Noraphamara bucked like a wild horse, chocking and gagging. Then it torqued its body forward, causing Max to slip off its back around to its front. The Noraphamara stood up with Max dangling like a pendulum from its neck. The creature tried to break free, but couldn't. Max wrapped his legs around the Noraphamara's ribs, locked his feet together, and squeezed. The creature gasped and wheezed, then fell to its knees with Max still clinging to its body.

Max then unlocked his feet and repeatedly kicked the creature with the heel of his boots while the Noraphamara struck Max's head with its palms. Then he planted his feet on the ground and sprung into a horse stance, simultaneously releasing the beast from the choke hold, tilting its head back, and executing a knife hand-strike to its throat. The Noraphamara collapsed on its side. Max leaned his back to the wall and looked down at the deceased enemy. "And kisses," he gasped.

Gigglis and Struthers had their blasters secured and ready for any other sudden attacks, while Bloomer covered the tail end.

"What's the status with our physicist?" Gigglis asked.

"Still in neverland, sir," Smitty said.

Gigglis activated his com-link. "We have K and Manning, over."

"Copy that, Lieutenant. Report to communications," Martin said.

"Will do, sir, out," Gigglis ended.

"Lieutenant," Bloomer called.

"Are you clear, Sergeant?" Gigglis asked.

"Negative, sir. About a dozen Noraphamara coming our way," Bloomer confirmed.

"Fuck!" Struthers blurted out.

"Move your asses, men, move it!" Gigglis ordered.

Bloomer shot his blaster in a rapid-fire pattern at the rushing Noraphamara. "Come and get some!" he shouted.

The others quickened their pace to a fast walk.

"Manning's dead weight is slowing us down," Smitty said.

"Try to wake him up, Corporal."

"Sir?"

"Like this, soldier." Struthers slapped Manning across the face. "Wake-up, Doctor!"

Manning shook his head after coming to. "Wha-whe-where am I?" He braced his head with his hands. "Ouch, me head feels like it was hit with a..."

"They're gaining, sir," Bloomer said.

Struthers aimed and fired.

"Move it! Move it!" Gigglis shouted. "Sergeant, you too."

"Sir, I could help..."

"Move your ass, soldier," Gigglis ordered. "Siddy, escort K and Manning to General Martin."

"Yes, sir."

The two Lieutenants stood side-by-side as they fired their blasters at the carnage that rushed towards them. "General, over," Gigglis transmitted.

"Report, Lieutenant, over," Martin returned.

"I sent Siddy, Bloomer, Smitty, and the two physicists your way, over."

"Understood. What's your twenty, over?"

"Section three in the mid-section of the sixth corridor, over."

"Keep..."

Static.

"...isn't stable... Will keep... over."

"Fucking com," Struthers said.

"General, you're cutting out. Repeat transmission, over," Gigglis said.

Struthers looked over his shoulder. His eyes bugged. "Oh shit!" he blurted as five other Noraphamara rose up behind them.

"Look out," Struthers shouted.

Gigglis quickly turned to Struthers. "How low is your crystal?"

"It's about drained and I only have one more E-crystal left," Struthers said and kept firing. "Are you good?"

"It's stable, but it has about had it and I'm out of crystals."

Struthers turned to Gigglis. "It looks to me like we're fucked."

"Stay positive, Lieutenant."

"I am positive that we're fucked, sir," Struthers said.

-9-

Labored breaths.

Deep sounding.

Why can't I open my eyes? Sara thought.

Inhuman breaths.

I feel weak.

Her eyes felt heavy, like tiny weights were injected into each lid. Sara hung suspended like a lifeless puppet with her hands tied together at the wrists, her arms raised above her head. Her wrists weren't cut by the stress of her weight, but were bruised. Her hair draped forward covering her face like curtains. Dirt caked over dried sweat and tears blemished her face. Her eyes were still closed, but soft whispers of breath escaped from her dry lips. Her eyelids slowly began to open.

My arms are so numb, she thought and lifted her head. Everything was a blur.

Why am I so... so...?

Her eyes focused.

Two Noraphamara stood before her; their eyeless faces fixed on her. They didn't move and they didn't speak. They just stood there. They were so still, so very still. Sara tried to shout, but she was too hoarse.

...help me... she thought, but the words could not come out.

"The lamb," a soft woman's voice said within the darkness. The soft voice was angelic to the mind, yet evil to the soul.

"Peecchhaatto, Noraphamara," the voice commanded.

The two Noraphamara kneeled, then bowed to Sara, but she was too weak and to scared to even ponder the action. The two beasts kept their heads down in respect. Respect for purity.

"Please God, help me," Sara softly gasped. *I feel...* she ended the thought.

Sounds of footsteps hinted in the shadows.

"I am your shepherd now," the voice said.

The footsteps came closer.

"Wh-who are you?" Sara asked, her voice raw.

"They can smell your purity," the voice said, "but will it be reckoned as a whore?"

And closer.

"Who...?"

"An angel of misery," the voice echoed in a whisper.

And even closer.

Sara felt cold, yet oddly at ease from the sound of the soothing voice.

Minda stepped out from the shadows and into the dim light, her movements haunting and graceful.

Then again, evil presents itself in the form of grace, Sara thought.

"Does my appearance please you?" Minda asked, with her fingertips skimming Sara's breasts.

Sara looked at Minda closely. *She is naked. Almost...perfect.*

"Answer me!" the witch demanded.

"No!" Sara said, but she was lying. "Wh-what do you want with me?"

"I want you to praise me with your cries," Minda said.

Sara struggled to get loose, but her bound wrists tightened to full numbness. "Let me go!"

Minda gently brushed her hand on Sara's cheek. Sara flinched. "What did you do to my father?"

Minda leaned to Sara's ear. "He's laid to rest, my child."

"No!" she cried. "God, please, no."

Minda stepped back. "Enough with your pretentious God," she hissed. "He means nothing to me!" She turned away from Sara. "Tiinnooa!" she commanded.

The two Noraphamara moved away from Minda and Sara.

"Let me go!" Sara screamed.

"No one hears you."

Sara shook her head as if saying no.

"Your father is waiting for you," Minda chuckled.

Sara didn't know what to say or do. She just hung there helpless and without words. The thought of what Minda said had fouled her mind like cancer.

Bloomer looked back and didn't see anything but torches on the walls. "So far, so good," he said.

"Keep running, Sergeant," Siddy gasped and took a breath. "We're almost there."

Keep running... keep running...

The right sleeve from Gigglis's uniform had been shredded to rags. The larger portions that remained were used as bandages to cover the lacerations on his arm. The Noraphamara's claws didn't sever any veins or arteries, but did make them visible. He tightened one of the blood-covered rags that were around his bicep. He gritted his teeth and grunted from the pain.

Struthers maintained his firing position while Gigglis cared for his wound. "You alright, LT?"

"I'm alive."

The Noraphamara began to deploy in masses. The majority attacked as others cannibalized their dead and wounded.

Struthers wanted to vomit from the sight. "God, that's disgusting," he gasped, but managed to keep it in.

Sounds of flesh ripping and blood slurping filled the two soldier's ears, even though they were at a distance. Squeals and shrieks soon followed.

"My E-crystal has about had it," Struthers said.

Gigglis fired his blaster. "We may have to resort to torches."

Struthers looked up at Gigglis. "Better to burn out, than to fade away."

...and they ran.

"Sara's gone, she's gone," Manning mumbled.

"We'll find her, Doctor. Don't worry," Bloomer said.

"No sweat, Doc. We'll find her," Siddy said.

With one swipe, Minda ripped Sara's suit, exposing

her black bra and a silver cross that rested just above her cleavage.

"False relics," Minda hissed. The chain snapped with no resistance when the cross was pulled from Sara's neck.

"Give it back!" Sara demanded.

The cross dangled from Minda's fingers as she looked at it then back at Sara. "Blessed are the sick, for they shall inherit the thirst." Then she tossed it aside. "Ah, my lost lamb," she continued, "there are no good shepherds."

Sara was silent.

Minda skimmed her index finger between Sara's breasts. "Ah..." she cackled. "My child."

"Don't touch me!" She shook from the cold touch.

"Fear not, your father is waiting for you."

"He's not dead!"

"I trust in my minions, my children," she whispered in Sara's ear. "I trust that blood was spilled. Your father's blood."

Is she lying? Is he alive? But that creature had him...what if she's telling the truth...what if she's right? Sara turned her head away from Minda and cried.

Minda turned to one of the Noraphamara that was to her right. "Xiix Qwweennma!" she commanded.

The demon wheezed at Sara as a twelve and a half inch insect that looked like a cross between a beetle and a camel spider protruded from its lower abdomen. The four-legged insect had a transparent shell, making its circulatory system and organs visible. There was a light blue tint to it and it squeaked as it protruded out.

Sara's eyes filled with fright and disbelief. She shook.

Minda turned back to Sara. Sara looked up at Minda and cringed. The Noraphamara approached Sara. The beetle didn't leave its master's hand. It waited.

"Get it away! let me go!" Sara cried.

"Shhhhh," Minda said softly.

"Let me..."

The beetle squeaked in anticipation.

"Let me go."

"Innards..." Minda interrupted. "…have an insatiable hunger for the flesh."

Sara eyes were baggy and bloodshot.

"The Innard begins its feast at the mouth..." Minda said while caressing Sara's face.

She then skimmed her fingers down Sara's neck. "It will binge your impure tongue to your larynx..." She continued down Sara's chest. "…then it will binge and digest your lungs to your heart. It will take its precious time."

Sara again pleaded for her life. "Please no..."

"Shhhh," Minda whispered while running her finger down to Sara's lower chest. "Then your liver to your intestines. Then it will end its feast by returning to your mouth to wait for its master."

Sara buckled her lips together and closed her eyes, hoping that it was all a bad dream.

Minda consoled Sara, wiping the tears from Sara's cheeks. "I'm your salvation, my child. Trust in me and you will never go astray," She cackled.

There was nothing Sara could do but cry. Minda stepped away from her, making way for the Noraphamara and its pet. Sara's eyes opened wide with horror.

The Innard jumped from its master's hand. But before reaching Sara's mouth, a pointed spinning object intercepted the beetle, jettisoning it to the wall. The Noraphamara shrieked in pain for its pet. Minda hissed and unsheathed her sword.

"Let the girl go!" a voice said. "I said, let her go!"

"Widower," Minda said and smiled.

Max entered into view. "Like I said before, you dumb bitch, let the girl go."

"Fiisstto Laaggaas!" Minda commanded, and the two Noraphamara rushed at Max. Max unsheathed his sword and dropped to one knee while simultaneously swinging and chopping the closest Noraphamara's leg off at the thigh. When the creature fell, Max stuck his blade in its back. He then quickly pulled out his .45 and fired two shots at the other Noraphamara's chest. Then Max aimed the .45 at Minda. "Let her go!"

The Noraphamara amputee grabbed Max's leg and jerked him to the ground. Minda rushed towards Max.

Max pulled out the other .45 and managed to fire a round, but failed to hit his target. Minda lunged at him with her arms raised in position. Max shot the Noraphamara twice with each .45, then aimed the pistols at Minda. He squeezed the triggers, but missed again. "You have got to be kidding me!" he said, and moved away from Minda's attack. The creature's claw was still attached to his ankle.

Minda sunk to the ground and buried three-fourths of the blade into the sand. Max quickly dropped one of the .45s and discharged the magazine from the other, replacing it with a full one. Before Max could aim and fire the .45, Minda slapped the gun from his hand.

"You're too soft, Widower. Your loneliness has made you weak."

Max rolled to his side as Minda attacked again, pulling his sword from the Noraphamara's back and severing the creature's hand at its wrist.

Minda kicked Max in the ribs and then swung her sword at his head. Max dodged the blade and retaliated by slicing Minda's leg. She screamed as her pus-colored blood ran. "The whore deserves to die like the four that possessed the power to oppose the prince." She looked down at her wound as she stepped back.

Max watched Minda's leg as her body regenerated the wound. *What the hell?*

"They're all dead," she cackled. "They're all forgotten."

Max lifted his sword and attacked Minda with multiple sword strikes; horizontal, diagonal, side-to-side, and center strikes. But Minda blocked every one and then retaliated back, but with an unorthodox style of swordsmanship. Max had difficulty defending himself from Minda's attacks even though he had studied the arts for many years. She sliced Max's right leg and arm as he hopped back.

Minda touched her breasts with her free hand. "Your unborn throbs for you," she taunted. "Do you remember the loss that you endured?" Her eyes gleamed with hatred. "Do you remember, love?" she cackled.

Max lunged at Minda and struck twice with his sword. Minda blocked both attacks. He then followed with a side kick to the ribs. Minda crouched as she held her side. Then he executed a roundhouse kick to the stomach. She gasped. He then swung his sword at her neck, but she parried and blocked the attack, and retaliated with a back fist to Max's head that knocked him backwards and into a slight daze. She lunged at him with a swinging sword aimed at his head. He parried the strike with his sword and retaliated with two swift strikes; one to her leg and the other to her ribs. He ended the attack with an uppercut to Minda's chin. Her head popped up and she stumbled backwards, but still she maintained consciousness.

"Fuck! Don't you ever fall?" Max said in a gasp.

Gigglis and Struthers ran through the fifth corridor that ended at a T. Five Noraphamara followed. Heavy thumps reverberated like the sound of Clydesdales with each step the Noraphamara took.

"Their gaining!" Struthers said.

"Keep running," Gigglis said.

"Which way? Left or right?"

Gigglis fired a round and it hit one of the Noraphamara in the shoulder knocking it to its side.

"Hard right."

They entered another corridor, a long corridor that seemed to have no end.

Static filled the com-link.

"...tenant Gigglis... physicists have arrived safely, over," Martin said.

"Sir, we copy, over," Gigglis returned.

"What's your twenty, over."

"Seventh corridor in section fifteen, over."

"Lieutenant, they're coming."

The two soldiers fired their last rounds.

"Fuck!" Gigglis said.

"This isn't good," Struthers added.

"Bloomer, Siddy and Smitty are on their way, over," Martin said.

"I don't think it's going to matter, sir, over," Gigglis said.

"Oh, why is that, over?"

"We're trapped at a dead end and Noraphamara are heading our way, over."

"This is it, LT. We're finished," Struthers said.

From a short distance the Noraphamara charged like cavalry with squeals, screeches, and roars as a verbal banner.

Struthers turned and noticed a big hole in the wall. "LT," he said, "I think the hole's big enough."

"Then move your ass, Lieutenant."

Struthers slammed the butt of his rifle at the top edge of the brittle opening to create a large enough entrance, then quickly dived into the hole. Gigglis pulled out a smoke bomb that he was saving to use for a joke on Bloomer's birthday. "This should buy us some time," he said, and lit the bomb and dropped it as he darted into the hole.

When the Noraphamara approached, the bomb released a pungent yellowish smoke into the atmosphere. The smoke irritated their sensitive skin, causing it to blister with gray liquid bubbles. As the smoke thickened, the creatures conditions worsened, their nostrils burned as mucus ran out from their mouths and nose slits. The creatures roared in agony and disappeared into the sand.

Minda trapped Max's swinging arm, wedged and torqued her hips to his, and threw him to the ground while following with her sword raised high. He wheezed but managed to retaliate with a snap-kick to Minda's abdomen. He then got up and rushed at her. She gathered herself before Max made contact, pivoting to the side and executing a roundhouse kick to his ribs. The kick landed flush, knocking the wind out of him. Minda then pivoted her hips and struck Max with a hammer fist to the back of the head that sent him to the ground.

"Why do you torture yourself?" she chuckled.

Max rolled onto his back to face her.

She looked down at Max with squinted eyes that glistened with hate. "Would you like the pain to go away?"

Minda looked at Sara then back at Max, and kicked him in the ribs, breaking what was already bruised. "The pain will never go away, Widower." She then pulled her blade from the sand and approached Sara. "Now you will miss another."

"Stay away from me, you twisted bitch!" Sara trembled.

Minda stroked Sara's tear-traced cheek and their eyes met. "Think of goodness, my child."

"Please no," Sara whimpered.

Minda's pointed her sword towards Sara's stomach, drew it back, and then stopped.

There was a muffled thud, followed by another. A cough, a gasp, and a... "God that hurt," Gigglis groaned.

"I can't breathe," Struthers coughed.

Minda turned and hissed at the interruption.

Max raised himself to one knee, using his sword as a crutch. "Now you have three to deal with," he said.

"Noraphamara Viivviiddoodda!" Minda commanded.

Then, five rising sand hills formed, followed by five squeals, to five deep roars, with five heavy breaths, and to five sets of teeth chattering. The soldiers were surrounded.

"Any votes, Lieutenant?" Struthers asked.

"Yes, one."

"What's that?"

Gigglis unsheathed his boot knife. "Always vote for the underdog."

Struthers squeezed his rifle with both hands like vice grips.

The five Noraphamara rushed at the two. Gigglis and Struthers yelled in war cry as they counteracted in a charge. Struthers hammered the charging Noraphamara's head with the butt of his weapon repeatedly until the creature fell to its hands and knees. He then pulled out his knife and sliced the creature's throat. Gigglis dodged one of the creatures and threw his knife at another as the blade sunk deep into its chest.

"Into the light, Lieutenant! Move into the light!" Gigglis shouted.

Minda looked back at Sara without saying a word and started to push the blade into Sara's stomach. The tip pierced through Sara's suit and into the skin's surface. Sara took an anticipating breath as she could feel the cold tip of the blade puncture the first two layers of skin. She then screamed as she felt the blade change its temperature from cold to hot.

Max ran towards Minda and Sara with his sword raised high. He swung the blade down and severed Minda's hand by the wrist. She cried in an awful screamed that pierced Sara's ears like a knife.

Sara watched Minda's hand and sword fall to the floor without blinking. Seconds later, the severed hand started to crack and change color to an ashen white as it broke apart into dust. Only the sword remained.

Before he could return with another strike, Minda slapped Max's sword from his hands, grabbed him by the neck and squeezed.

"Take my flesh; I take your life," Minda said.

"Your hand doesn't make us even," Max gasped. "You owe me!"

Minda tightened her grip just enough for Max to see white fuzz fill his eyes and dropped him to his knees. He gasped and coughed while rubbing his neck. Minda picked up her sword and sheathed it. She watched as her own blood slowly regenerated a new hand. Sara couldn't believe her eyes.

"My life will not grant you peace, Widower," Minda said. "It will only ordain your sadness as just." Her eyes slanted to a squint. "The fact is, Widower, your life belongs to me."

Bloomer and Smitty entered the room and fired at a Noraphamara that was about to attack Struthers.

Minda looked up at the two soldiers, then returned to Max. "My job is complete," she said. "There is no future for you."

Minda unsheathed her sword and cut Sara free.

Sara fell limp next to Max.

"My gift to you, Widower," Minda said before she vanished into the darkness.

Seconds later, the Noraphamara followed by disintegrating into sand, leaving their dead behind to rot.

"They're gone," Bloomer said.

"I thought..." Struthers panted. "I thought we'd about had it at any moment."

Max helped Sara to her knees, but she was too weak to move on her own.

"I was so scared, Max, but I… I couldn't move. I couldn't…" She began to cry. "I'm so sorry, Max. I didn't..."

"I didn't either," he said while raising her to her feet.

"Is my father okay? Is he safe?"

"Your father's fine."

"I want to see him."

"Soon, Sara."

"Why am I so weak, Max? I..."

"Shhhh, don't talk."

The soldiers gathered around Max and Sara.

"Is she okay?" Struthers asked.

"She'll be fine," Max said.

Soon after in the communications room, Sara's eyes filled with tears of happiness as she held her father tight.

Max met with General Martin to make sure that everything was up and going: transmissions were on line, life support, etc. Thereafter, questions were brought to Max's attention, but the only thing Max could tell the General that he was sent by the council.

Shortly after regaining long-range coms, Martin transmitted an S.O.S. to the Eve colony. Reinforcements had been sent to make a clean sweep of the area, as well as the Cydonian land itself. There were no signs of the enemy, only the dead that were left behind, those which later had been set afire and burned to ash.

Back on Earth: Arizona.

Sara stepped off of the Vortex gangway and placed both feet on the ground. She watched as the horizon changed to dusk and took a deep fresh breath. She looked back at Max with a soft smile, her face slightly bruised.

Max smiled back. Her eyes never left his. Sara brushed Max's stubbled face with her fingertips. Her eyes lowered. "I don't know what to say, Max." Her eyes gazed up at him. "I don't have the words, but only..." She smiled. "…thank you."

He looked at Sara with a soft yet despondent look. "I don't have the words either."

"Max, why did you?"

Max's eyes held Sara's, knowing what she was going to say. "I wanted to give you a chance that I never had."

Sara looked puzzled. "What do you mean?"

"A chance to save a loved one," he said with a broken smile.

Sara didn't ask, but she could see the pain in his eyes.

Max cupped his hand to Sara's.

"Did you lose something, girlie?"

"My cross. Where..." She paused. "It's very special to me. It was my mother's. It's been somewhat..." Sara then reversed her hand over his. "Now I give it to you," she said. "Even though the chain was snapped, it might be able to help you."

Max knew what Sara meant. *Thank you,* he thought, but didn't say it. "I have to go now, Sara."

"I know." She looked up at the night sky. "Will I ever see you again?"

"Maybe someday."

Sara hugged him tightly. "Good-bye, Max."

"Take care of yourself, Sara. Be safe."

Minutes later, Sara opened the driver's side door to her Jeep. She could hear the Vortex's thrusters engaging as the ship lifted off. Swirls of dust erupted from the ground while the spacecraft lifted into flight. She watched the Vortex while wondering if she would really ever see him again. *There are good shepherds*, she thought as the Vortex diminished into a dot of light in the peaceful night sky.

DeparturE

"What was designed for peace resounds in emptiness, and with one single breath the future people of all worlds... forgive us, for we are the founding fathers of the emptiness."

-The Teacher

Four days later.

The deceased soldiers who had given their lives for their planet and galaxy were shipped back home to Earth and were buried at Arlington National Cemetery. Drops of rain fell and splashed into tiny beads that ran down the dozens of extended umbrellas suspended over the heads of those assembled. The smell of brisk drenched air and the freshness of blossoming flowers embraced the morning. Families and friends grieved while fellow officers paid their respects with a salute. Some officers held back their tears; others tried. The flags that covered the seventeen coffins were neatly folded in triangles and were handed to the soldiers' wives or children.

Martin gave the eulogy. "...and with pride, these brave men who served and sacrificed their lives to protect all mankind will be forever missed. Now we say good-bye to our comrades, brothers in arms, and dear friends. May they know they are always a part of a family that extends beyond what is transient, a family all its own. The Corps."

The twenty-one-gun salute echoed through the cemetery while *Amazing Grace* played on bagpipes from a distance. There were seventeen bagpipes in all.

PART TWO

TragedY
&
TyrannY

-10-

Planet, Xissba
M-33 Galaxy: Scorbic Star System

Clouds of thick smoke hovered over the distant horizon like black curtains. A soft-spoken breeze brushed through the fields of decomposed grass and ruins like a ghostly hand. The thick smoke suffused with a robust scent of freshly scorched flesh and decay. In some parts of the land, the smoke became fog, a fog that was the result of a demonic sideshow. A sideshow that was not to be taken lightly, but meant to render order by punishment for one's sins; sins of choosing anti-elegance to the new era and one's own belief over the beliefs of the Demonixa.

Kneel before me... The words were spoken. And the people were branded the sign upon their foreheads. Hopes and dreams diminished into ashes by one spoken name: Oroan-in translation, *Demon of the Eclipse*. A name that breeds terror into the hearts of all Xissba people: a nonviolent race of beings who have greeted their sorrows with bleeding knees; stripped of dignity, freedom, will, and life. There was a new order, a new era.

Three-fourths of the Xissba race had been restrained in death camps like cattle and others put to death as their families watched. The cold-hearted act of execution.

Miles away at Camp Torpid Inanimate, the rancid smell thickened to a putrid stench that burned the noses of new arrivals that were not tamed to the foul scent. Some tried to hold their breath or cover their faces with clothing while others vomited. Some cried; mostly confused children. Others, such as mothers and fathers, held each other tightly for the fear of losing one another, The people that had no one to call their own prayed in mourning whispers, while some stood silent filled with fright and confusion. Hundreds of Noraphamara chaperoned the newcomers like watchdogs.

The steel gates opened and the wind blow to a chill.

As the new arrivals entered into Torpid Inanimate, the people noticed five black Noraphamara: two to select for experimental torture, and the other for death. The three other Noraphamara were part of the selection as well; two to hold the individual by the arms while the other branded the man, woman, or child's forehead with the sign, (the Demonixa symbol) and were put to use as slaves.

The new arrivals were herded in. And the selection began. *And let thy cry come onto thee.*

Some of the old arrivals stood and watched while others looked in the opposite direction. A family of three: father, mother, and a little girl, entered. The father was taken to be branded, he was then pushed to the side.

His wife cried for her husband; the little girl held her mother's hand tightly with one hand while the other held an old and tattered doll that her mother had given her years before. The child called for her father, "Pahpah, blinstoo na... Pahpah!"

The mother was next and was separated from her daughter. The little girl held to her mother's hand, but then was taken away. She struggled against the Noraphamara, but she couldn't break free. "Nali, ne tatant," the mother shouted to her little girl in gloom as she was about to face execution. "Mahmah, tatant, Mahmah. Maaammmaaa!" The little girl dropped her doll as she was dragged to a room nearby for experimental torture. The little girl's father picked up the doll and held it in his arms as if he were giving his child her last hug, then fell to his knees and cried for his family.

A Noraphamara cackled.

From a short distance there was an old arrival named Toosoo who saw the grieving father and quickly walked towards him. He knelt beside the father. "Come with me, new arrival. Come." He assisted the helpless man to his feet.

"They're gone," the father cried while leaning his head down on Toosoo's shoulder. "Gone."

Toosoo consoled the new arrival while they promptly walked away from the entrance and into the crowd.

"Their souls will not diminish into darkness. Remember that," Toosoo said.

In some cases faith is hard to come by in times like this, but here it's all you have.

Toosoo took the new arrival to an old, weathered-down shack, which had no entrance door to it, and a medium-sized slit for a window that was across the way. At least it was away from the spotlight.

The minutes seemed like days as the selection was still in progress, yet the lines began to dwindle in mass. The new arrival sat in the dark staring blankly at the outline of his daughter's doll. The lids of his eyes were reddened and puffed.

Toosoo watched slaves carry unclothed lifeless bodies that were put in piles nearby. Most of the bodies looked like skeletons covered in skin with their eyes half opened. Some had burns that were so bad they were unrecognizable to the loved ones who carried them; some had deep lacerations to the skull; some had their arms and legs twisted to a curl; some had their eyes picked out with only the bloody sockets remaining; and others had their arms still tied to their backs and their thumbs stretched or ripped clean off the hands. They all had unmerciful deaths.

Toosoo's eyes lowered for a brief moment. He could hear the new arrivals plead for their lives as they were entering the camp. *So much death; so little peace.* He then returned to watch the slaves. *The madness and the sacrifices I see.*

But still, he watched. *I was told not to interfere, but...* And he kept watching.

The slaves themselves looked malnourished. Body frailty and mind fatigue plagued the camp, lingering like a sickness.

"The enemy has grown strong," Toosoo murmured. "Too strong it seems."

There was nothing, only softly held back breaths of sorrow.

Toosoo turned to look at the new arrival's dark outline and sat next to him. They sat together in silence.

Elsewhere on the planet.

The room was ice cold, and reeked of a morbid aroma: a mix of unrelished sulfur and rotten meat that burnt the nostrils, leaving a bad taste. The room smelt like death. Dimmed with black candles that had been placed randomly around the area, the blood red flames flickered above the melted crowns like dancing devils possessed in rhythm. Some would speak of foreseeing one's death while looking deep into the dancing flame. But who knew for sure? No one, they were all dead. And with each death, the flames would become thicker and brighter, yet the room would never become fully lit. Evil cloaked the full brightness of light like a thick haze, leaving only a hint of what lay beneath, what lurked in the shadows.

The flames were red flickering waves of blood. A black figure shadowed in an outline sat at his throne in triumph with his head rested back and with his snow white eyes narrowed to a gleaming slant. Thick traces of breath released from his mouth like a humidifier, the vapors were wet and cool as they slipped from his lips and into the cold pungent air.

Carnmassicre's generals sat at opposite sides of the room in thrones. There were six generals, all from different origins. They were known as the ghosts of war.

The double doors opened. Minda entered the room and kneeled to one knee before Carnmassicre with her head bowed. The generals whispered to each other like gossiping devils.

"My Prince, I have..."

"Failed!" Carnmassicre's voice was deep with an accent of wisdom.

The generals abruptly ceased their gossip.

Minda looked up at Carnmassicre, but only saw his white eyes and a black outline within the throne. "I beg forgiveness, my Prince," she pleaded.

"Forgiveness is neither a privilege nor a right, for you are the last of my flesh and blood."

"I am beholden by your decision, my Prince." Minda bowed and then stood to her feet.

"This planet's liberation falls short and pales compared to the power of Demonixa culture," the dark prince said as he addressed the others, "for this is the beginning of a new era, a new tribulation. My Generals, you are the standard bearers of the Demonixa. It is you who are my extending hands of tyranny. So speak on your behalf."

"We must strike and take over this world completely, leaving the last remaining city in ashes," a general said.

Carnmassicre nodded in approval.

Minda gave a hidden smile while looking at the general who had spoken.

"It's been said in a rumor from the starbase Intrepid, that a Human/Manduurin attack on the Demonixa is imminent, my Prince."

"The Manduurin are weak as their ancestors. That is why they allied with the humans. Yet they posses the Eclipse as well, so they will have to be dealt with by crippling their resources and their military power," Carnmassicre replied.

"What's our next move?" another general asked.

"The crown of worms has been put upon the heads of the Xissba people, for the end is imminent. It is a plague that envelops the land like locusts, a pestilence of their faith. Where is their God now?" Carnmassicre cackled. "This world and its people belong to me."

Minda looked up at Carnmassicre. "What is your bidding, my Prince?" she asked.

"Summon the Rekluse and their riders, and send them to Xilla, the last free city of this world." Minda slowly nodded. "The attack will begin at first moon rise," Carnmassicre commanded.

"As you wish," she relished, and walked away.

"And, Minda."

"Yes, my Prince?"

"I want Xilla left in ruins."

"Do you want survivors?"

The dark prince leaned forward. His skin was like Minda's, which stretched over his well-defined physique, testifying to his strength and power. Although unlike Minda, he had no hair, only solid white markings that covered his scalp in a collage of patterns. They were demonic tribal markings indicating his mastery of the black arts. His eyes narrowed. "I want them all dead." Then leaned back in his throne. "I want the slaughter to be a feast for the Rekluse."

"As you wish." She bowed once more before leaving the room.

"What do you bid of us, my Prince?" another general asked.

Carnmassicre raised his hand and a hologram of a planet appeared in the middle of the room. His eyes narrowed. "Go to the planet Lurrane. It is the eighth planet of this three star system." He moved his hand in a half circle.

The hologram revealed the starbase Intrepid, which had been docked with starships that rotated the planet's orbit. "And here's the starbase you spoke of, General."

The general nodded.

"It is no longer a rumor, General," Carnmassicre continued. "This is the time to cripple the enemy by severing one of their vital limbs."

"What do you suggest?" a general asked.

"I want that starbase and all its starships destroyed, and..." Carnmassicre's white eyes glazed over with a hypnotized gaze, "I want the planet eclipsed."

"Yes, my Prince," the general said.

Carnmassicre lowered his hand and the hologram vanished from sight. "The attack will begin at the second moon rise."

"As you wish," the generals said, and all six of them vanished within their thrones and into the shadows like spirits.

Carnmassicre sat back with a wide stare as if he were in a trance of some sort, with traces of breath escaping from his lips. "Yes, as I wish," he said.

Camp Torpid.

Some time had passed and the first moon was about to rise. The first moon was always a harvest moon; it was large and orange-colored with a light red glowing aura around it. The people of Xissba believed that the first moon was the sacred eye of Kridgneel, the God of new beginnings, (the orange represented peace and goodwill, and the red aura represented the halo of great life and growth), the second moon, the new moon, would follow shortly after, and would shine with a white brightness (the white represented purity).

It had been hours since the selection had passed; it was dark out with only stars to shine upon the sorrows and suffering that had occurred. The stars were a sign of hope for the Xissba people, but hope dwindled with each life that was taken. Alas, the stars fell down with the bodies. Even though the camp was quiet, the sadness remained. From a distance there were cries from children who held their motionless loved ones in their arms. Others huddled together sheltered only by blankets near mini-bonfires.

Toosoo tried to stop himself from crying, yet he couldn't hold back the tears that filled his eyes. *They all had names*, he thought. *Why was I chosen, and there's nothing I can do to help these people*. "I have to escape and tell the others of all that I've seen." He turned to look at the new arrival. "What's your name?"

The new arrival hadn't moved from where he was as the doll still rested in his hands. He looked up at Toosoo with tear-reddened eyes. "Higgli," he said.

Toosoo lowered his eyes, smiled and returned to look out the opening. "Nice to meet you, Higgli."

"What's your name?" Higgli asked.

"Toosoo," he said.

"What land of Xissba do you come from?" Toosoo asked.

"Xsaa. And you?"

"I'm not from here."

Higgli looked at Toosoo with puzzlement. "But you look like a Xissban."

"Yes, but this is only a mask, not my real appearance."

"Then who are you? Where do you come from?"

Toosoo looked away from Higgli and continued to peer outside. "I'm from a distant world that was eclipsed by the Demonixa many years ago. My people are all but extinct, only a few remain in hiding; no one knows we still exist. Not the Demonixa, nor our younger decedents."

"What is this eclipse you speak of?" Higgli asked.

"It is a weapon that blackens planets, killing every living thing. Even the planet's core perishes from the effect. My people are to blame for this mass destruction and it's our sadness to bear."

Higgli Stood up and approached Toosoo. "Why do you say that?" he asked.

"My people, with help from the Teacher, developed the Eclipse weapon. It was used to destroy the planet Icubin during the first tribulation. Morgmordeus called it *a new era*. It was a time of fear and death..." Toosoo paused. He looked up at the orange moon. "After the demise of Morgmordeus, the murderous king of Icubin, the weapon was dismantled; never to be used again. But we made a mistake. The history and schematic of the Eclipse was engraved on the walls in a temple in Manduurin hieroglyphs. We did not think that the Demonixa could decipher our cryptic writings."

Higgli accompanied his gaze. "Peace and goodwill they say, Toosoo, with the halo of great life. Do you know what it really means?"

"No."

"We believe the peace and goodwill comes as we

live in body and peace within ourselves towards all life."

"As for the great life and growth?" Toosoo asked.

"Great life in the afterlife and the growth of spirituality."

"My people believe similar to yours."

"But our beliefs are what put us in this situation," Higgli said.

"What do you mean by that?"

"The Demonixa presented themselves as a good race and they wanted to help us with our resources." He looked down at his child's doll and squeezed it until his hand shook. "We had no idea this would happen."

"How could you? The Demonixa have many faces to disguise only one, and it's evil. You're race is not alone, Toosoo. There are other races with many planets destroyed. And my people suffered the same fate as well."

Higgli had nothing to say in return, but he knew that he had someone who could relate to his situation and his unforgettable loss. And in a way, Higgli knew that Toosoo suffered the same loss, one way or another. And in a way Toosoo was reliving that loss, but in another's eyes.

Not far from Camp Torpid.

The ground caved, leaving dozens of large sinkholes scattered over the land's surface. The holes were deep and the insides were neatly shaped funnels with openings at the ends. Dirt slid down the funnels like miniature landslides as long pointy legs protruded from the holes. Second's later, large arachnid-like insects dug their way out from the holes like sand crabs. The creatures' transparent exoskeleton displayed their interior bodily organs. When eating its prey, the remains could be seen moving through their digestive systems like squirming worms until all the pieces were liquefied.

Inches away, the surface around the area rose with dozens of six and a half foot hills that formed black and florescent yellow striped Noraphamara. This type of Noraphamara differed from the others. Their skin had a hard carapace shell-like skin that acted as a suit of armor. Two horns pronged out from the back of their eyeless heads and forked just above their nose slits. Their claws and teeth were slightly longer than the average Noraphamara demon. The yellow blotchy stripes symbolized blood rank between the large groups. Some had stripes that covered their muscle-bound torsos; some had stripes on their arms and hands; some had stripes from the top of their heads to the small of the backs. On worlds past, these creatures were known and feared as the Sucturamara. The demon riders of war.

A chorus of howls, squeals, and chirping sounded from the Rekluse as the Sucturamara hopped and mounted the large arachnid creatures. The Rekluse hunched their backs as they quickly moved across the terrain.

Camp Torpid.

Toosoo and Higgli walked towards the main gates.

"Do you hear that?" Higgli asked.

"Yes," Toosoo said.

The chirping. The odd sounds of movement.

"W-what is it?"

The howls. The squeals and screeches.

Before Toosoo could answer, the six-legged creatures rushed across the way. “The Rekluse and their riders, the Sucturamara.”

“I’ve heard of the Rekluse and the Sucturamara, but I have never seen them.”

Toosoo looked at Higgli. “I wonder where...”

“Heading northeast to Xilla,” he murmured.

Toosoo nodded. “May the good spirit have mercy on their souls, for the Dark Prince has come.”

“We should head back to the shack,” Higgli insisted.

“It’s time,” Toosoo said.

“Time? Time for what?”

“My time here is finished, and I want you to come with me.”

Higgli looked puzzled.

“War is approaching, Higgli. We leave tonight.”

“Leave? How are we going to do that?”

“I have to return to my people, so that I can find the Teacher,” Toosoo said.

“Who is this Teacher you speak of?” Higgli asked.

“If I can save one soul from death, I want it to be you.”

Higgli gave a warm smile. “We leave tonight.”

Later that night.

Toosoo and Higgli crawled through an underground water drainage tunnel on their hands and knees. Traces of mud and sand collected on the floor of the tunnel, while thin scattered streams of water flowed in patterns under them. In time, the two escapees struggled their way through the tunnel, as mud and sand thickened while they crawled further on. Now the mud and sand was up to their hips and shoulders. Higgli paused briefly to check to see if his daughter's doll was still tucked safely in the waist of his pants. He exhaled in relief and continued on.

As they reached the end, Toosoo and Higgli headed northwest to the Xiriin mountains. With caution, they ran to the fields.

-11-

Planet Talia: 5/5/2090

Milky Way Galaxy: Gleera Star System.

Hours had passed since Max's arrival. The Vortex's modifications were taken out and the Polaris type 2 sphere was sent to be analyzed for any changes. At the general physics lab, Dr. Tillin-Vii looked over the Polaris data carefully. After the data log was completed, animated pictures appeared and were downloaded to a file disc. The pictures were chopped and were out of sequence, but still the information was an important addition to the prior data log. The pictures had been collected from the visual system in Max's helmet. The Polaris type 2 sphere was a phenomenal piece of equipment, an enigma of its kind. After the information had been recorded and filed, Dr. Tillin-Vii then sent the information to the Council.

Later that day, at the N.E.C. (Nattal Embassy Council), Max stood patiently in the hallway looking out a window while waiting to meet with the Council. He looked up at the peaceful midday sky. Clouds brushed across Lake Prill, leaving white reflections over the clear blue water. A flock of four-winged birds, known as Blinarings, soared in a triangular pattern across the way. Their feathers were blended shades of blue on their back and wings, the lighter shades led down to the belly of the body and wings that brushed to a solid white. Their heads were a dark blue with white streaks above the eyes and a long slender beak. The birds were at a distance, yet Max could hear their multi-pitched chirps. The peaceful view eased Max for the moment. That moment was short-lived. The door opened to the high senates meeting room and a soldier in gray BDUs walked out. "Sir, the Council will see you now," he said.

Max walked in. The room had white walls with twelve flags hanging upright. The flags represented each council member's planet and country. The Council was made up of six selected leaders from Earth and six selected leaders from other worlds: three Manduurin from the eclipsed planet Egypuun, one from the race called Pleerod from the planet Plee'Lera, and the last two members from a race called V'Nall that were from the eclipsed planet Lipnou. The council members sat at separate judicial benches, which had the symbol of the Corps on the front. It looked like a courtroom to Max, with twelve judges in blue clothing with black trim. Max also saw five generals sitting at a table on the other side of the room: Brigadier General L'Rovmed (Plee'Lera), Major General Svoo-Maa (Egypuun), Lieutenant General Rayland Martin (Earth), General Keith Masters (Earth), and five star General Jonathan Kipling (Earth).

"On behalf of the council, we thank you," one of the Pleerod council members said.

"Glad to be of help," Max nodded.

"We've viewed the recorded data, Mr. Leer," another Pleerod council member said, while holding the data files in his toggled hands. "And I see that there were twists and turns per se. Granted, the mission was an unusual one, but you managed to come through."

"General Kipling has informed us that you declined compensation for your effort," one of the human council members added.

"That's correct. What I did had to be done and it would have affected not only me, but other worlds, perhaps other galaxies, as well. Besides, the Demonixa had to be stopped."

"Yes, and they were stopped. At least for the meantime," a V'Nall council member said.

"What are the chances of this happening again?" Max asked the V'Nall councilman.

"No idea. We were lucky to have come across this information when we did. We may not be so lucky next time."

"But we do have Carnmassicre's whereabouts," Gen. Kipling said.

"He has inhabited Xissba, correct?" another human council member asked.

"That's correct, sir," Kipling returned.

"We have been carefully monitoring Demonixa's activity for months. Many countries on that planet have been eradicated or have been enslaved. It's time to act, now that we know where he is."

"Agreed," said one of the Pleerod councilmen. "The hourglass runs thin. And as for fleet status?"

"A third of the fleet has been sent to starbase Intrepid. The U.S.S. Mayflower and U.S.S. Aurora will be shipped out the day after tomorrow to meet with the rest of the fleet," Gen. Masters said.

"Good."

Max cleared his throat to get everyone's attention. "Excuse me, but is it a good idea to send a third of the fleet?"

"Mr. Leer, the council believes that sending a third of the fleet will become an advantage that may end this war," one council member replied.

"Yes, in theory," Max said. "The enemy is very strong. But in order to defeat them we must trust them, and by trusting them we must understand them."

"How can you say that we should trust the enemy?" a council member asked.

"Trust that they will be consistent. I know that peace is never achieved by any means but war. But that doesn't mean..."

"We appreciate your input, Mr. Leer," a council member said.

"The council has to reconsider the game plan," Max continued.

"Thank you, Mr. Leer."

Max hesitated.

Hours later.

Max walked out and saw Anom Lawrence looking out the window. He turned to see the open door. "Nice day, isn't it?"

"I thought I was supposed to look you up."

"Yeah, well, I wanted to save you the trouble."

"I see."

"So, how was your debriefing?"

"Educational," Max said in a flat tone.

"Did you get a medal or a certificate of appreciation, or perhaps a free dinner at the steak house?" Lawrence rubbed his stomach. "Now that's fine dining, if you ask me."

"It was a verbal medal of appreciation."

Lawrence patted Max on the back. "And that, my friend, is the gift that keeps on giving."

"They also asked if I would re-enlist."

"Was that before or after the debriefing?"

"After."

"And?"

Max walked to the window. "I said that I would think about it." His facial expression was pensive. His right arm was resting on the wall as he stared blankly out into horizon.

"Are you alright?"

Max didn't answer.

"Max?"

"I'm fine," he said in a low tone.

"Are you sure? You look troubled."

Max hesitated.

"It's Emily, isn't it?"

Max continued to look out the window. "I thought about going back to save Emily and my sister before returning."

"What stopped you?"

Max looked at Lawrence. "I don't know."

"There could have been good or bad repercussions if you had gone back, but then again, there are laws and gridlines."

"The thought had crossed my mind once or twice."

Max returned his gaze to the lake, but there were no Blinarings flying across the water like before, only the soft tides that rippled from the breeze. "It's been eight years, but I just can't get rid of this pain, this loss... and the thought of that long unsaid good-bye. When I confronted Minda, the feelings were unbearable. I was angry; my mind was clouded, my center was gone. I'm surprised I didn't fuck the mission, or get myself killed."

"Do you still have the dreams?"

"Almost every night, and if I don't dream about Emily or Jessica, I dream about Minda. It's like I'm bewitched by that..." He paused and squeezed his fist. "I shouldn't be..."

"Max, look. You're human. What I mean by that is, your life has been interrupted by a tragic..." Lawrence paused for a moment. "But you have to be at peace with yourself and I know that it's easier said than done. If not for yourself, do it for Emily. I know you would want her to do the same if she lost you." He placed his hand on Max's shoulder. "I hate to see you like this, Max."

"I'll be fine, Anom."

"I know you will, my friend."

"I get this way sometimes, that's all."

"Whenever you want to talk, I'll be here."

"Before I forget…" Max reached into his inside pocket and pulled out Anom's incased penny. "Thanks for the luck. It helped."

"Hey, what are friends for? Friends are supposed to look out for each other."

"Indeed they do."

Max and Lawrence started to walk.

"I thought you didn't believe in luck?"

"I don't," Max said. "Don't I owe you a snake bite or two?"

"Or three or four," Lawrence said with a sly smile. "I have some time before I ship back to the Milky Way."

"Do me a favor," Max said.

Lawrence could see the concern on his friend's face. "Sure. What is it?"

"Whatever happens out there, keep your center."

"I will. On Emily's honor, I will."

Planet, Lurrane: Starbase Intrepid

M-33 Galaxy: Scorbic Star System

There were three knocks at the door of Fleet Admiral Hanson's quarters.

There was no answer.

Three knocks were repeated. Hanson awoke and sat up in his bed. He looked at his watch and yawned. It was 04:10 a.m.

The knocks continued.

"One moment," he said as he put on his robe.

The door slid opened. "Ensign," Hanson greeted, his voice slightly groggy and his eyes half open.

The navel officer stood at attention and saluted. "Sorry to wake you, Admiral, but you didn't answer your com."

Hanson rubbed his eyes. "What is it, Ensign?"

"You have a deep space transmission from N.E.C., sir. It's General Kipling."

"I'll be right there," Hanson yawned.

"Aye, sir," the officer said.

Hanson buckled the top buttons of his uniform before entering communications. "Ensign," he said.

"Sir, General Kipling is ready for your reply."

"Visual."

"Aye, sir."

Kipling came into view. "Greetings, Admiral. How's the weather?"

"So far, so good, General," Hanson said.

"Anything exciting?"

"Haasmel's comet is making its pass through the area, and a mild chance of a meteor shower later this evening. And you?"

"Sunny and warm."

"That's good to hear. What can I do for you, General?"

Kipling leaned back in his chair. "The council has given the approval for the first wave air strike. You may attack at any time."

"Sounds good, General, but I think it would be wise to wait. We only have one flight line crew here, and a majority of the Typhoon Migs are not fully armed yet. I wouldn't want to chance it, at least until the others arrive," Hanson said.

"Agreed. The other crews will be aboard the Aurora when she and the Mayflower arrive, so hang tight."

"Sounds good, General."

"Were you informed of other squadrons arriving?"

"Yes, Rear Admiral Xee-Laau had given me a list of all aircraft and pilots before he left the Intrepid."

"Good. General Masters and..."

Static abruptly filled audio and fuzz slightly covered the visual screen. "General, your transmissions is breaking. Could you repeat that?"

"General Masters and I will meet with you and Vice

Admiral Marshall when we get there. I..."

The transition began to chop to where Kipling's appearance and speech were unrecognizable."

"General, I may have to get back with you later. Our..."

"...then we'll attack in..."

The transmission chopped.

"Ensign, clean up that transmission," Hanson said.

"Trying, sir, but the transmission is being altered somehow. But I don't..."

Kipling's transmission was severed and the visual screen blanked.

The ensign paused when he saw the long range censor screen. "Sir, I'm picking up Wraith fighters approximately sixty-two meters east of Lurrane's moon and closing."

"Wraith count?"

"Sixty-two thousand," the ensign said as he continued to push buttons. He turned to the admiral. "The count is rising."

"A giant cluster," Hanson murmured. "Sound the alarm."

"Aye, sir."

Hanson folded his hands behind him and watched as the little black dots accumulated into a large mass on the censor screen. "It seems that the battle has come to us."

-12-

Alarms blazed and pilots rushed to their Migs. The flight line crew scattered to each fighter like wildfire as they rushed to fuel the first squadron of ships. There were fifty-two Typhoon Mig squadrons in all; twenty percent of them had been dead-lined for repairs and or needed to be armed. The odds were not in their favor and chances were slim.

Time was ticking.

The enemy was near.

The first wave was done; their thrusters roared and they took off into the battlefield. In a short time, the second, third, and forth waves had joined the first squadron in a thump thrusting roar.

"I need fuel for Mig twenty-six!" one flight line crew member shouted.

"Coming," another returned.

"I've got a fuel leak on Mig twenty-eight!" a voice shouted.

"Skip it and move on," the lead crew member shouted.

Migs twenty-eight, twenty-nine, thirty-three, thirty-five, and thirty-seven had to be dead-lined for repairs.

The ships either had a ruptured fuel line, a fried sensor chip, or a bad thruster relay switch connection. It wasn't the best of days for the flight liners, but they managed to send out the majority of the squadron in good time. The docking bay trembled from fusion cannon bursts.

One after another, cannons fired at random. Wraiths exploded and imploded into debris, but more came. With each fallen wraith fighter, another would take its place. Wraiths always attacked in large groups, their thrusters at a chorus. That was what made them so intimidating, so frightening, and so very deadly to their enemies.

A triple explosion occurred as three Wraiths attacked the east fusion cannon; two fighters were hit to make a diversion while the other acted as a torpedo and broadsided the double-barreled cannon. There was nothing left but a black crater.

"We've got kamikazes! Watch it!" a pilot said.

"Roger that," a voice responded.

"I see them," another said.

Wraiths separated into twenty large clusters that were scattered all over the battlefield. The only thing that the Mig pilots could see were the florescent red trim that outlined the Wraiths' outer hull.

"Squadrons six and seven regroup," a voice said.

The remaining Migs of squadrons six and seven merged together into a large V-pattern. The other squadrons were still scattered and were in packs of two, stopping other kamikazes from penetrating through.

"Stick to your wing-man," a pilot said.

"Mig twelve, check your six!" a pilot warned.

"Rog..."

But it was too late. *Another pilot had fallen.*

"Three Wraiths, at two!" a pilot said.

"Dammit! Five Wraiths have just slipped through."

"I've got 'em."

"Don't worry about them..."

"Mig ten, check your two."

Like jolts of red lightning, four Wraith fighters fired rapidly at the defending Mig until there was nothing left but dust.

Another fusion cannon had been hit. *It was another kamikaze.*

Wraiths swarmed the area like locust and flanked the Typhoons at all sides. Migs scattered like gnats being swatted by a large hand.

"They're everywhere!"

Other Wraiths headed for the Intrepid.

Fusion cannons fired at all directions. There were six cannons left, and the count was dropping. Wraiths rammed themselves at the Intrepid's hull, while others fired at vital spots, like the docking bay doors, communications tower, and the remaining six fusion cannons. Two large explosions occurred in a second's time. There were now four fusion cannons left.

Wraiths then attacked the ninety-two starships that were dispersed around the Intrepid. The Wraiths did not fire at the docked starships, but acted as torpedoes toward the E.S.S. class destroyers and then U.S.S. carriers. The majority of the ships were either unmanned or unprepared. Sixty-three starships had been hit and were engulfed in flames. There were no survivors. Multiple explosions occurred and then implosions. Thick clouds of black smoke hovered at a standstill.

The defense was thinning; the offense had thickened.

The alarm continued to blaze. The hallways were filled with scattered personnel.

"I repeat, all personnel, evacuate immediately and report to docking bays sixteen through thirty-seven," a female voice said over the com.

"Admiral," Captain Steelborn called. "I suggest you accompany me to the Prowlburn."

Hanson nodded at the starship captain.

"Vice Admiral Marshall will be accompanying the E.S.S. Boone."

More explosions from the outside continued. With each blow the Intrepid took, its inner hull trembled and began to weaken.

"U.S.S. and E.S.S. starships, prepare for departure. I repeat. All U.S.S. and E.S.S. starships prepare for departure," the female voice announced.

The walls were starting to crack and the floor weakened from the intense heat from the deck below.

"Look out!"

"The floor..."

Hanson and Steelborn looked back, but it was too late. The floor split open and fire burst out as if it were the gates of hell. Horrifying screams escaped from the mouths of the victims that were swallowed by the flaming chasm. Hanson and Steelborn made a mad dash down the hallway before the split could reach them. The walls cracked open and coughed out a black thick cloud, followed by water spraying out from ruptured pipes. In minutes, half the deck collapsed and disappeared into the fire.

Outside of the Intrepid, the ships disembarked from their ports; E.S.S. ships were the first to leave the harbor. Like flies to a meat house, Wraiths continued to bombard themselves at the moving targets. Ships that were in free flight fired their cannons just so they could break free from the swarming circle. Or was it a swarming cluster? No one knew for sure what it was, but what they did know was that they had to get out in one piece and protect Lurrane from the inevitable.

Wraiths scattered away from the cannon bursts, but some were not as fortunate and were caught in crossfire.

"Get them away from the ships!" the commanding pilot said, as Wraiths circled around and fired rapidly at the starships' cannons.

Migs maneuvered through the cluster by the tips of their wings.

"I lost my wing-man. I..." a pilot said. "I… I'm loosing fuel. Debris must of..."

"Your right thruster's on fire!" a pilot warned.

"To your right!" another shouted.

Three Wraiths fired upon the crippled Typhoon and hit the rear and the cockpit.

All that was left was the midsection of the fighter.

"Keep your eyes peeled, and watch your wing-man," the commanding pilot said.

"Roger that," a pilot replied. "Check your three," he warned his wing-man as four Wraiths were heading their way.

"I see the bastards," the wing-man returned. "I'll go high and you go low, and then we'll meet in the middle."

"Roger."

The two Migs went their separate ways; one Wraith went high and the other three went low.

"What the hell?" the wing-man said with a hint of envy. "Why did you get three?"

"I have no freaking idea, but they're on my ass like a zit," the other pilot said.

The two Migs circled back and headed towards each other as if they were heading for a dogfight.

"A second before we meet, make a hard right," the wing-man said. "On my mark."

"Roger."

Wraiths were gaining closer.

"Steady."

"I'm steady, and ready."

"Now!"

The two Migs jerked to their right. The thrusters boomed as they created a vacuum effect, sucking the four Wraiths into a collision. After the implosion occurred, the debris scattered forcefully out from the vacuum. The Migs maneuvered out of the way of the sharp shooting objects. One of the pieces of debris pierced through a passing Mig's left thruster, but it didn't explode.

"I'm hit!" the Mig pilot shouted. "I'm losing fuel, and fast."

The left thruster failed, "Shit!" and then the right.

"Does anyone have a band-aid handy?" the pilot said, just before...

Out from within the cluster of battle, a badly damaged Wraith swirled out of control and headed for the Mig.

"Tommy, eject! Eject!" a pilot said.

It was too late. The Wraith impaled itself in the Mig's cock-pit and was obliterated, decapitated from its free-floating wounded body.

"Shit," the commanding pilot blurted. "Watch for debris! We don't need anymore casualties."

"It's everywhere!" a pilot said.

"Check your two, and your three," another pilot warned.

"Got 'em," the other responded.

"Bloody bastards! They almost nipped my bloody wings," one pilot growled.

"You have one on your tail, Johnny."

"I can't shake the bastard." The pilot zigged then zagged, then went up, then down, but the Wraith would not desist. "Get this asshole off my bum."

"It's a little hard when you're moving like you're drunk, Johnny."

"Well, bloody hell!" Johnny said.

Captain Charles Reed stood up from his chair and pulled out a handkerchief from his left front pocket, then dabbed the sweat from his forehead. "Magnify visual," he said.

"Aye, sir," Lieutenant Tara Brown acknowledged.

Reed's eyes widened from what he saw.

It was the Enmity; the second largest war ship of the Demonixa Navy, (the largest was the Ismodeus, which was not present at the battle). The Enmity was the equivalent size of six large cities, (it was ten times the size of any E.S.S. and U.S.S.) and like Wraith fighters, the Enmity had a glistening black outer hull with florescent red trim that outlined the intimidating vessel.

"They're going to eclipse the planet," Reed said.

First officer, Commander Kara Walsh, walked to the helm. "Lieutenant, what's the exact distance of that ship?"

"Hundred and twenty thousand kilometers and closing, Commander," Lieutenant Brown said.

The bridge trembled. Walsh and Reed struggled to maintain their balance; the other crewmen were safely planted in their seats.

"Damn Wraiths!" Reed blurted in frustration.

Walsh looked at Reed. "Wraiths are the least of our worries."

"Captain, our three rear fusion cannons have been decommissioned," Lieutenant Junior Grade Bailer reported.

The bridge shook again, but this time it wasn't as violent a hit. It was more like a shock wave from an explosion. It was another starship, the U.S.S. Billo.

Marshall entered the bridge. "Captain, report."

"Admiral, we've lost three rear fusion cannons and the Enmity is on its way."

Marshall folded his hands together behind him.

"We believe that the Enmity is planning to eclipse Lurrane," Walsh said.

"Any sign of the Ismodeus?" Marshall asked.

"No, sir," Reed said.

"Ensign, open a channel to the U.S.S. Prowlburn," Marshall said.

"Aye, Admiral," Ensign Xii-Luun said. "Channel open."

"Captain Steelborn," Marshall said.

"Steelborn, here."

"This is Vice Admiral Marshall."

"I see that you made it on board alright, Admiral."

"Yes, I did. Did Admiral Hanson make it?"

"Yes, sir. Admiral Hanson is on his way to the bridge now."

Reed turned to Xii-Luun. “Open a second channel to Starbase Primestrill.”

“Right away, sir.”

The implosions were getting closer and closer.

Cmdr. Walsh could see the mass destruction from the visual screen. Her head turned with her eyes closed briefly. *All the lives gone. Friends gone. What else is there to do, but run? Flee for our lives*, she thought.

“Captain, Primelin is not responding to our transmission,” Xii-Luun said.

“Damn!” Reed said to himself, his teeth slightly clenched. “Keep trying. Open other channels if you have to. Do whatever it takes to get through to that starbase.” He began to rub the bridge of his nose with two fingers, but the tension was still there.

“Yes, sir,” Xii-Luun said.

Reed looked over to Marshall. “Admiral, I’m sorry to say, but we may have to retreat on this one.”

Marshall stood quiet for a moment, then nodded at the captain even though disappointment overwhelmed him from the decision that he made.

“Admiral Marshall,” Hanson’s voice came over the com. “What’s your status?”

“Not good, sir. We’ve detected the Enmity at an approximate distance of twenty-two thousand kilometers. And we’ve lost...”

“Hundred and ten thousand kilometers, sir,” Brown said.

“They’re going to eclipse,” Hanson said.

“That’s been a concern, sir,” Marshall replied. “With over half of our fleet gone, we may not have a chance of stopping the Enmity from eclipsing Lurrane.”

"We must..." Hanson's transmission chopped abruptly. "…while we have a chance. What..."

The Prowlburn shook. Its outer hull was weakening from the vibrations of Wraith bombardment. There were two ways around it. *Do or die*.

The Prowlburn is a tough ship, yes she is, the captain thought.

Migs were still out there, in the heat of one big cluster fuck of a battle, and they were about to be extinct. The crew stumbled as they recovered themselves from the attack that had just occurred.

"Admiral, your trans... chopped. I don't..." Marshall's voice scattered.

"Dammit!" Hanson spat. "End transmission."

"Ensign, open a channel to all squadrons," Steelborn said abruptly.

"Aye, sir, right away," the ensign quickly replied. "Channel open."

"All remaining squadrons, this is Captain Steelborn. Retreat to the U.S.S. Prowlburn and dock…"

The bridge trembled, like a large wrecking ball had just slammed through the ship's hull. The crew could hear the inner hull shift and bend.

"What the hell?" Lieutenant Baxthorn coughed.

"Lieutenant, report," Steelborn said.

"Decks five and six have been breached with bombardment," Baxthorn said.

"Close those two decks out."

"Sir, more Wraith heading our way," Baxthorn said.

"Fusion cannons full spread."

Wraiths retaliated by thickening their attack: some discharged rounds as others acted as torpedoes. The enemy was determined to destroy the last carrier.

"Ensign, open a channel to the Boone," Hanson ordered.

"Aye, sir."

"We may have to retreat, Admiral," Commander Fii-Naa said.

"Channel open."

The com spat out chopped words and sentences with a touch of static.

"Your transmission's breaking," Marshall said.

"Sir, the Prowlburn is sustaining heavy damage to its outer hull," Brown reported.

"It's a sitting duck," Walsh said.

The alarm was activated.

"Captain, one more direct hit to the engine compositor and the Polaris sphere is going to rupture," Baxthorn said, while routing access pressure from the Polaris to the compositor. And time was running out.

"Admiral, Capti... get... abandon ship!"

It was too late. The bridge was silent as the crew watched the inner hull of the Prowlburn light up in a bluish-white explosion. "What the hell just happened?" Marshall said.

"The Prowlburn's Polaris sphere ruptured," Brown said.

"The ship looks dead," Walsh said in amazement. "I-I don't. My God." The vessel itself was still intact. At least for the moment.

Wraiths fired at the condemned vessel, (there were no kamikazes). The Prowlburn caved like brittle wood and crumbled into floating dust, separating into the open void of space. There were neither bodies nor anything that represented the inside of the succumbed ship, as all had evaporated with the Polaris rupture. There were now only four ships left: the E.S.S. Boone, Musoshi, Hammern, and the Sun Tzu.

"Sweet Jesus. I've never seen anything like it," Marshall said with a flat shocked tone.

"Neither have I," Walsh said.

"Captain, Wraiths heading our way," Brown said.

"Weapons status?" Walsh asked.

"Front and mid-level cannons still operational, Commander."

Reed stood over Xii-Luun's shoulder. "Any luck, Ensign?"

"Negative, sir. I've tried different channels and nothing. I believe the Demonixa are jamming our long range transmissions."

"Can you encrypt the transmission into different code formats and send them automatically through random channels?" Marshall asked.

"Yes, sir, I believe I can," Xii-Luun said, "but it may take some time."

"You have ten minutes, Ensign."

"Understood."

Walsh stood behind Brown. "What's the Enmity's position?"

Brown turned to look at the mid-range sensors screen. "Eighty-seven thousand kilometers and closing, Commander."

"Mig status, Lieutenant?"

"Eight... no wait, now there's seven, Captain."

"Is your reserve bay free, Captain?" Marshall asked.

Reed nodded. "Ensign, open a channel to all fighters."

"Right away, sir."

Xii-Luun's hands moved swiftly over the com console without overriding any encrypted codes. "Channel open, sir."

"All remaining Migs, this is Captain Reed. Retreat to the Boone and dock at east bay."

"Roger that, Captain. We're coming in," the lead pilot returned.

"Captain, we have an incoming transmission from the Hammern."

"Patch it though," Reed replied as he sat down in his chair. "Captain Schneider, what can I do for you?"

"Did Admiral Marshall make it on board?" the German captain asked.

"Yes, I'm here, Captain," Marshall confirmed.

"Any ideas on how we're going to get out of this?"

Before Marshall could speak, Brown turned to Walsh and said, "Wraiths are retreating." He then returned to his console. "This doesn't make any sense?"

"This isn't good," Walsh said.

Reed gazed at the screen. "They're getting ready to eclipse Lurrane."

The Enmity's engines hummed with a deep purr that had a vibration affect that surrounded the afterburners. The sound was daunting to any who heard it, for it meant that they would soon be touched by the hand of shadowy death, The Eclipse.

The Captain sat in its command chair with its arms propped at the rests like a puppet. Its skin had a rust brown tint to it with thin hoses at the crown of its head, which connected to the arms, back, and chest. Its face only exposed two nose slits and red eyes that flickered like fire. The mouth was absent, but when it spoke, a mouth would appear and move in slow motion. Its name was Klattamattu. In translation it meant *Captain of the star-filled underworld.*

There were only two Klattamattus in existence, and the other commanded the Ismodeus. Like its dark prince, Klattamattu showed neither mercy nor compassion. Its life, its mission if you will, was to lead the second largest force of Wraith fighters to ever invade the cosmos. The Klattamattus were created and used to bring devastation and great terror to any race that opposed Carmnissacre and his new era.

And now, another example has to be made, the Klattamattu thought, with its red flickering eyes subsiding to a blood red shade and then to a cold milky white.

"Soon to be in position," the star charting minion announced.

The bridge was lit by control consoles and a viewer screen which revealed the planet Lurrane and its demolished starbase. Klattamattu didn't move nor speak, but waited until it was time to give the deadly command. And it was near.

Wraiths were in position. Klattamattu could see the four E.S.S. ships approaching. It was quiet and it waited. Its eyes returned to a blood shade; the coloration trickled in miniature globs of red like two heated lava lamps.

"In position," the star charting minion said.

The two piloting minions hovered their hands over the lighted console. The Enmity slowed to a stop; its engines decreased in power. *It was time.*

Klattamattu leaned forward from its chair and its face formed a grotesque lipless mouth. “FIRE!” it commanded with its mouth stretched in a feral grin.

-13-

"Engage fusion cannons, and fire!" Marshall commanded.

All four starships unleashed their cannons at the moving target, knowing what might happen, but that was a chance Marshall was willing to take.

Wraiths retaliated by sacrificing themselves to the fusion blasts. Implosions increased with each added burst that was discharged and the Eclipse was untouched. The time had come.

Forgive us.

Reed rushed to the weapons console. "Target war heads at the Enmity at these coordinates. Fire at will!" he commanded.

Sixteen nuclear warheads screamed from their silos. Each missile had a flag decal at the base of it. The flags were of the United States, Germany, Japan, and China. These four remaining countries were the last to represent freedom, protection and tranquility to all life forms. Wraiths, this time in pairs of three, intercepted the missiles by ramming them head on in a suicide ploy to protect their mother ship. The explosions and implosions were much more devastating than before, creating bluish-white holes that swirled into nothingness, sucking any Wraith that was near into its event horizon.

But all that didn't matter, because the planet Lurrane was about to look the demon of the Eclipse straight in the eyes. Oroan had spoken one word for it: *death.*

"It's too late," Walsh said. Her words were softly spoken.

A bright flash glared then dissipated into the planet's surface. A fraction of a second later, the eclipse raised its ugly head with a loud thundering roar that caused the planet to quake. Minutes after, a sheet of black death crept over the surface of Lurrane, enveloping all light and life on the planet. Lurrane was now at its end and was assimilated into the dark abyss.

Forgive us.

All four starships vibrated from the aftershock.

"Captain, the Enmity's charging its weapons," Brown said.

"Ensign, any word on Primestrill?" Reed asked.

"Sir, I'm getting a faint signal from the starbase."

"Clean it up!"

"I tried, sir, but I'm not having any luck."

"We don't have time. We must retreat. There's nothing we can do now," Marshall said.

Reed shook his head.

"Captain, the Enmity's full charged."

"Navigator, quickly chart a course to the Xubaala star system and relay it to the others," the navigator nodded.

"Polaris sphere is on line," Baxthorn said.

"Course charted, sir," the navigator said.

"Event horizon in five... four... three... two..."

Each starship created its own vessel-sized wormhole. The holes were white with light blue streaks that resembled fresh running water. The streaks were trails of stars at the other side of the horizon. To the survivors, they were a lifeline.

As the ships entered the horizon, the Enmity fired its deadly cannons, but the four ships escaped and the holes closed. The Enmity's bursts bolted through the never of space, and the soul survivors of the battle of Intrepid were now in the warm open arms of a safe haven.

The starbase on the other hand, which had been Lurrane's protector for nearly two decades, was not as fortunate. Moments after the wormholes collapsed, the Intrepid's outer hull cracked and crumbled into rubble that flaked into the voids of space.

Carnmassicre's image appeared on the viewer screen. His eyes gleamed with power.

Klattamattu bowed its head at him. "The planet is eclipsed, my Prince."

"And the Human/Manduurin starbase?"

"Destroyed."

"Excellent."

"My Prince, four ships escaped our attack."

Carnmassicre didn't show any facial expression of anger nor disappointment.

"Forgive me, my Prince," Klattamattu bowed.

Carnmassicre's eyes turned flat white. "The survivors will return and others will come to follow, for they will see their future's end at the hands of the second era. Gather your forces and return to Xissba."

"Yes, my Prince," Klattamattu replied.

Carnmassicre raised his hand and the transmission ended.

AftermatH

"The shadow of darkness has found its home in the name of madness... and its home will forever be its salvation."

Founding Fathers of the Eclipse

Silence is the only unspoken word that escapes the lips of infinity... as innocence falls.

Oftentimes, reality forms in a blink of an eye.

A vision of a brave new world had been extinguished, and all hope with it. All that was left of the Intrepid was a skeleton of smoke and scattered debris. Fragments of destroyed starships surrounded the base like the rings of Saturn. Bodies that were sucked out floated lifeless into the never and were capped in ice. Their eyes missing, only frozen blood sockets remained from the after affects of compression. The once almighty Intrepid was now a space burial ground.

From a distance, Lurrane's moon rotated in tragic disbelief, cracked and left in shadow, unseen from its mother's shell.

The surface of Lurrane had become clay, and all plant and wildlife were gone. Not only did the surface suffer, so did the inner core, becoming brittle like yoke to the egg.

On some areas of the planet, large sinkholes morphed into city-length craters, infused with the bodies of the citizens of Lurrane, their faces contorted from the pain and the loss of their souls departed. Structures slumped like bowed candles, cracked and withered in black. The atmosphere was gone, except for the deep gray clouds which created an eclipse winter over the planet. Perpetual snowflakes fell and the planet became ice cold. Black snowflakes.

Eventually, the clouds would dissipate. The snow would stop, and the planet would harden and crumble away into nothing, followed by the core. Only then, the moon and the Intrepid's skeleton would remain.

Silence was the only unspoken word that escaped the lips of infinity as innocence fell. Sometimes reality forms a tear in a blink of an eye.

PART THREE

ThE DroP (DeatH FroM AbovE)

-14-

Earth's Moon (Starbase Lupus)
Milky Way Galaxy: Delta-1 Star System

"Do you know what the high priority is about?" Commander Anom Lawrence asked.

"Not a clue," Captain Kevin Teple said.

Teple and Lawrence entered the briefing room and saw four officers standing together in conversation.

"Captain Teple, Commander Lawrence," Admiral Tinnara greeted.

"Admiral," the two officers returned.

"Have a seat, Gentlemen," Tinnara said. "Captain Shelby and Commander Franks will be joining us shortly."

The six officers sat around a large round table that had a medium-sized triangular-shaped transmitter in the middle. The entrance door opened and Capt. Carly Shelby and Cmdr. Todd Franks entered.

"Sorry for the tardiness, Admiral," Shelby said.

"You're just in time, Captain. Have a seat."

"What's the high priority, Admiral?" Teple asked.

"I asked Generals Kipling, Masters, and Rear Admiral Xee-Laau to join us this morning to discuss our present situation."

Teple and Lawrence looked at each other.

"Situation, sir?" Lawrence asked.

Admiral Tinnara pinched the bridge of his nose with his fingers. "We've taken a heavy blow to our fleet," he said. "Our resources are at a standstill."

The officers were in shock and the room felt like it was caving in.

"My, God," Lawrence murmured. *Max was right! He knew what would happen. He knew.*

"Are there any survivors?" Teple returned.

"Only the Boone, Musashi, Hammern, Sun Tzu, and seven Typhoon Migs survived the attack. Everything else is gone."

"Did Lurrane sustain heavy damage?" Shelby asked.

"It was eclipsed shortly after the battle," Laau said.

The look of helplessness overwhelmed Captain Teple. He then closed his eyes and looked away. "Is the council aware of this, Admiral?" Franks asked.

"Yes, they are," Tinnara said. "And they're aware that they've made a mistake."

"Mistake?" Lawrence questioned.

"Commander," Teple said.

Anom paused. "With all due respect, Admiral, this wasn't a mistake, it was a slaughter. The council had to have known that."

Laau raised his hand. "Yes, Commander, we know what it was, but there's nothing we can do now."

"But to retaliate," Tinnara said.

"Will we be meeting the Boone and the others at Primestrill?" Teple asked.

"No. They're heading here as we speak."

Teple looked at Tinnara oddly. "Sir?"

"Primestrill was hit before the Intrepid."

"When did this happen?" Shelby said.

"We don't know," Laau said. "The transmission was sent just minutes prior to their destruction."

"A lot of casualties and a lot of lives unaccounted for... too many," Masters said.

Tinnara leaned back in his chair. "Captain Teple, you will be leading this battle."

"Understood."

"Colonel Willington of the 908th Airborne Division will be aboard your ship. The Division will be separated due to space, so you'll have half of the Division and forty-two shuttles with you. They may need air support shortly after their arrival, so brief the Badger squadron before shipping out."

"Understood."

"Are the Scorpion Voughts about ready?"

"Yes, sir. We're waiting for the next armory shipment, which is due tomorrow."

"Good to hear, Captain," Tinnara then turned to Shelby. "Captain, you'll be transporting the other half of the Division, the other forty-two remaining shuttles, and bombers."

Shelby nodded. "The halo and the Bombardier squadrons are preparing as we speak, sir."

"Excellent," Tinnara said. "And ship status?"

"ZB-1 Bombers and the B8 Infiltrators are about up to standards," Shelby informed.

"Very good," Tinnara eased. "The M.S.S. Nightingale will be with you to aid the wounded."

The briefing went on for hours and it seemed like days.. After reviewing the transmitting image of the planet Xissba and the Demonixa's whereabouts on the planet, they decided on a plan of attack that would hopefully give the Corps the upper hand, and perhaps win this war.

Shortly after, Teple and Lawrence were the last to leave the room, and with an odd feeling of bewilderment.

"This isn't good," Lawrence said while unbuttoning the top two buttons of his uniform.

"I know," Teple said. "I think the council underestimated the Demonixa's full potential."

"I don't think this attack was the Demonixa's full potential."

"Perhaps not, but we have forty-eight hours till we find out."

"Will that give us enough time to get the remaining fleet ready?"

"I hope so. If not, we all might as well kiss our asses good-bye."

The two officers stopped at the end of the hall and waited for the elevator doors to open.

The elevator beeped, the doors opened and six other officers walked out.

"Captain, Commander," they said.

Lawrence nodded.

"Good afternoon," Teple returned.

The doors closed behind the two officers.

"Level four," Teple said. "The 16th infantry Division

should reach Xissba by tomorrow and that should give us some time till the 908th get there. Let the pilots know they have a twenty-four hour pass to see their loved ones, then report to the Mayflower at 01:00 for briefing before deployment."

"Aye, sir. When will the 908th be briefed?"

"The colonel gave them a twenty-four hour pass and then they'll be briefed."

Lawrence nodded.

"I'll be meeting with General Kipling and Colonel Wellington within the hour to discuss the mission."

"Will I be needed, sir?"

The elevator doors opened.

"No." Teple walked out. "Take the rest of the day off and relax. We're going to have a long day ahead of us."

"Sir?"

"Report to the Mayflower at 06:00 tomorrow."

"Understood, sir. See you tomorrow."

"Bright and early, Commander."

The doors closed.

"Level twelve."

Later that night as Lawrence was enjoying a relaxing evening in his quarters, he received a deep space transmission from Max. Lawrence was pleased even though he had talked to him two days before. But it didn't matter, Max was Lawrence's most trusted friend; his only true friend. More like a brother. "How are you?"

"Max?"

"Doing well. And yourself?"

"As cool as the wind in the Rockies." Lawrence leaned back in his chair. "I'm about to hit the hay though. I have a long day ahead of me tomorrow."

"I know."

Lawrence gave Max an odd look. "You know?"

Max gave a sly smirk. "Did I ever tell you that I have great mental powers, and I can read minds and see the future?" He wiggled his fingers like a stereotypical hypnotist. "Look into my eyes and you'll be in my power... forever," he laughed.

Lawrence chuckled. "Seriously, how did you know?"

"I heard what happened to the Intrepid, and I decided to..."

"You're re-enlisting?"

"I volunteered for special Ops."

"Volunteering means enlistment, my friend."

"And I did."

"I'm glad you're back."

"Me too."

Lawrence looked disappointed. "I'm sorry I'm not going to be there with you, like old times."

"Don't worry about it, Anom. You're needed on the Mayflower."

"I know. But I still miss the field. Can you blame me?"

"Not at all. I'm shipping out soon and I'll be there by tomorrow."

Shortly after the transmission ended, Lawrence lay on his bed with the lights out and his eyes open. His mind was elsewhere, but it wasn't enough to ease his eyes shut. He lay there bright-eyed and restless, listening to the clock and counting the ticks. At a minute past the hour, his eyelids became heavy and drooped.

The next morning at 05:58, Lawrence entered the bridge of the Mayflower where he would meet with Teple. The bridge had personnel at all posts as they performed ship diagnostics, Polaris diagnostics, weaponry checks, and navigational uplinks. Teple was at the weapons' console with Ensign Dickerson as they discussed the ship's weapon modifications.

"...and how much time will that take?"

"Two or three hours tops, sir."

"Good."

"Good morning, Captain," Lawrence greeted.

"Did you get enough sleep last night, Commander?"

"Yes, sir."

"Good to hear. And the long day begins."

"Are the Voughts ready?" Lawrence asked.

"Not yet. They've been dead-lined until armory..."

"Captain Teple," a voice said over the bridge's com.

"Teple, come on."

"Sir, armory has arrived."

"Be right there."

"Aye, sir. I'll let them know."

"Well, speak of the devil."

"All in good timing. You have the bridge, Commander."

"Aye, sir."

Hours later in the officer's room, Captain Teple, Commander Lawrence, and Colonel Wellington were discussing where and when the air strike might be needed. A format of Xissba was displayed on an overhead screen that was at the back wall of the room. Death camps were marked and all Demonixa hideouts were targeted and most importantly, the battlefield, the arena of the unpredictable.

There was a beep at the door.

"Come in," Teple said.

The door slid open and Sara Manning walked in. She handed Teple a digital map chart and stood before him across the table. "Captain, the star charts you requested."

"Thank you. Any progress on your course charting?"

"Yes, sir, the course was charted and was relayed to the other navigators when they arrived."

"Very good, Ms. Manning," Teple complimented. "Now if you will excuse me, I have a captains' briefing to attend in fifteen minutes." He stood up from his chair and turned to his first officer. "Commander, when Max Leer arrives on Lupus, please escort him to the Mayflower to his quarters before his briefing with General Kipling and Colonel Wellington. His ship will be docking at port twenty-six." He looked at his watch. "He should be here within the hour."

"Aye, sir," Lawrence said, then looked over to Sara. He could see the excitement and anticipation in her eyes, knowing what Max had told him was true. But he didn't know what kind of feelings she had for Max. Maybe they were strong. *And if so, why for so long?* he thought. Lawrence excused the question and headed out of the room. Sara followed.

"Excuse me, Commander," she said in a slight hesitant tone.

Lawrence stopped. "What's on your mind, Ms. Manning?"

"I… I know it might sound funny, but I would..."

Lawrence smiled slightly. "Funny, Ms. Manning?" But he knew what she was hinting.

She cleared her throat and smiled. "Do you know Max? I mean how..."

"Sara, take a breather. Breathe in; breathe out. I know Max very well. I've known him for many years now. And I think he'll be thrilled to see you."

"I would like to accompany you to Lupus to meet with Max."

"One condition."

Sara was slightly confused. "Commander?" she said.

"Max likes to be surprised."

Sara remembered the last time she surprised Max, and to her surprise it followed with the barrel of a 45. "Well when..."

"Trust me, Sara. Surprise."

"He may not even remember me. It's been twelve years."

"But for him, it's been a day. Trust me, he remembers you, but he doesn't know you're here. That's what makes it a surprise."

"I see," she said while reminiscing in thought.

They walked to the elevator doors while they talked about how she and Max had met.

Lawrence found it to be very interesting, and yet kind of odd. *But a good odd I suppose,* he thought. "And you've thought about him all this time?"

"Quite often, I'm afraid."

"Scottish lassies happen to be his cup of tea, you know," Lawrence imitated in accent.

"You don't say," he said and smiled.

The Vortex's gangway opened minutes after its landing. Coolant vapors brushed out from the exhaust couplings as the thrusters cooled and regained pressure. Minutes later, Max walked out and saw his friend Anom Lawrence standing in front of the gangway with his hands folded behind him.

"How was your trip?"

"Ten hours too long."

Lawrence looked up at the Vortex and noticed its battle-damaged outer hull, and shook his head.

"You know, Max, you really need to fix the ole' girl," he said. "Her hull needs care."

Max looked up at his ship. "She does need some attention, doesn't she?" he agreed.

The two old friends shook hands and hugged.

"When do we ship out?" Max asked.

"The day after tomorrow. But before we go any further, I have a surprise for you," Lawrence said.

Max shook his head and smirked. "You have a what?"

"It's been a long time, stranger," a familiar voice interrupted.

Max turned to see if the voice behind him was...

Sara had a smile that could light up a midnight sky; even her eyes reflected from the grin.

She is even more beautiful, Max thought. But he couldn't tell her that.

"It's so nice to see you again, Max." Without thinking, Sara hugged Max and squeezed him lightly.

Was it more of a reaction or had it been intentional? She didn't care, because she had been reunited with the man who had saved her father years ago.

Max returned the hug. "It's good to see you too, girlie."

Lawrence placed his hand on Max's shoulder. "We have to continue the reunion on our way to your quarters. I'm sorry to say this, but time is limited."

Max nodded. "Shower and a shave sounds good right about now," he added, while rubbing his stubbled face.

When they arrived, the door to Max's quarters slid open. Max walked in, then Sara and Lawrence followed. "Your ambassador's suite, my friend," Lawrence said.

At the far end of the room sat a navy blue couch with a glass coffee table in front of it. A glass chessboard with its pieces lined in formation rested on top of the table. Near a large window sat a plain oak desk with a flat screen monitor for incoming and outgoing transmissions. To the far right of the room was a bed with navy blue sheets, a pillowcase, and a comforter. To the left of the bed was a door that led to the bathroom and a large walk-in closet. An oak dining table with two chairs facing each other acted as the room's centerpiece. That's where Max placed his gear.

"Thanks, but isn't this a little much?" Max said.

"The Corps is really happy that you're back."

"Yeah, okay."

"Just look at that window. It's so big," Sara said.

Max glanced at the window. "And…"

"And you have a great view," she said.

"Of…"

"Space."

"Exactly," Max said and shrugged his shoulders.

"I hate to break up the space debate, but we're not able to stay and chat," Anom said.

Max nodded. "When is my briefing with the general?"

"In three hours, in the captain's conference room."

"I'll be there."

"You should try to get some sleep," Lawrence said.

"I'll try, but if I can't, at least I have this big window to occupy my thoughts," Max said.

Sara smiled at Max and then followed Lawrence out the door... and the door slid closed.

-15-

Beads of water dripped from the shower as steam hovered and the mirror fogged with droplets of sweat. The shower curtain slid open after a brief pause. Flight Captain Rhiannon McLachlan held her breath as she wiped the excess water from her face and wrapped her shoulder-length strawberry blond hair with a towel. She then used her hand to wipe the mirror free of mist.

On the streaked surface that remained, she saw the blurred reflection of a blue-eyed stranger; the same blue-eyed stranger who always appeared behind the mist and between the streaks; the same stranger who always stared at her with hollow questions that had no answers. Rather than indulging in another game of who will blink first, she reached for her robe, exhaled deeply, and walked out of the room.

As she made her way through the hallway and entered the living room she heard beeps coming from the transmission monitor. “Transmission received,” she said.

The monitor activated and a young woman with reddish hair that hung down to her cheeks appeared.

“Good evening, Sis,” the young cadet greeted with a smile.

Rhiannon gave a look of disappointment. "Oh, Cathy, your graduation. I'm so sorry. I..."

"What's with the sad face? Its okay, Sis," Cathy said abruptly. "I heard about what happened, and I know you've been busy and I understand that. Besides, you were with me all along." She smiled and placed her hand over her heart.

"That means a lot, Cathy," Rhiannon returned.

"Aye."

"How was your graduation?"

"It went well. After the ceremony we received our orders."

"So soon?"

"Aye. Colonel Lii-puu will be instructing us on the new fighters. Our training starts tomorrow, and then we'll be shipped out in two weeks."

"I've heard that the Corps has been developing a new fighter."

"As I remember, the colonel calls it the FB-1 Specter; the most advanced fighter in the fleet."

"You don't say? Did Mum and Dad show up?"

"Aye, and they said that they miss you very much."

Rhiannon picked up a picture of her mother and father from her nightstand that was near her bed. "I miss them, too. Are they there now?"

Cathy shook her head. "They took a shuttle back to Scotland this morning."

Rhiannon kissed the picture before putting it back on her nightstand. "I'll see them soon."

"When do you ship out?" Cathy asked.

"09:00 tomorrow."

"Is your squadron prepared?"

"Aye. I made sure of it. It'll be our sixth mission, but they're still a bit nervous. But I don't blame them though. I'm a bit nervous me-self."

"You'll do fine, Sis. You're the best squadron leader the fleet has, and some day I hope I'll be as great as you."

Rhiannon gave a hopeful smile. "Thanks for the encouragement, Cathy."

"I don't have much time, but I have to ask."

"What is it?"

"Any news?"

"News?"

Cathy lifted her brow. "You know what I mean."

"Are you talking about Commander Lawrence?"

"Uh-huh, the love of your life."

"Don't you have a class to attend?"

Cathy smirked. "No, not at the moment. Now tell me."

"Fine," Rhiannon sighed. "There is no news."

"Did he give up on you?"

"No, I don't think so. As a matter of fact, he tries even harder." Rhiannon's eyes wandered for a moment. "In fact, I find it a bit flattering."

"Then what's holding you back? You like the commander, right?"

"Aye, I do, but..." Rhiannon paused.

"Is it because of his rank? And I know it isn't his looks. His brown eyes, his black hair, the little dimple on his chin… Must I go on?"

"I don't know what's holding me back. When I'm ready, I'll let him know."

"Look, Rhiannon, go where your heart takes you and you'll see. You have nothing to lose, and a lot to gain."

"Maybe."

"Sooner or later you'll have to face the black stairs, ye know."

"Aye."

"And when you do, I'm going to give him a pep talk."

"No, don't do that," Rhiannon pleaded.

"I'm sorry, but no one is going to date me big sis without a pep talk," she said while pointing her finger at the com-screen.

"We'll see."

"Well, Sis, I've got to go now."

"Aye, I know. Just take care of yourself, okay?"

"You too." Cathy's eyes widened. "Oh, before I forget, remind Catalina she owes me a tennis rematch."

"I will," Rhiannon said.

"Hey, are you okay?"

"Yeah. Why?"

"You just seem a little distracted," Cathy said.

"I'm fine," Rhiannon said and smiled, even though she knew it might be the last time she would ever see her little sister again, but her mind couldn't give in to the negative.

"I love you, Sis."

Rhiannon lightly touched the com-screen. "I love you too, Cathy." And the screen went blank.

Later that evening on Earth.

Stars glimmered over the South Carolina horizon

and fireflies fluttered their wings, landing on trees and bushes, glowing like green Christmas lights. *I couldn't ask for a better evening,* Flight Lieutenant Catalina Broomfield thought, as she took a deep breath of the cool gentle breeze, which smelled of the fresh summer night. She tucked herself closer into her boyfriend's arms with her hands folded over his, and sighed in comfort. She looked up at him and paused, like she was about to say something.

"Are you comfortable?" Benjamin asked.

Catalina nodded. "I just don't have the words for the way I feel right now."

Benjamin pulled her closer and kissed the top of her head. They both returned their gaze to the stars.

"I ship out tomorrow," she said.

"I know, and there's nothing I could say or do to change that," he said, "but I'm okay with that, because I know you'll come back."

Catalina knew that there was a chance that she might not come back, but she didn't want to ruin Benjamin's hopes. "When you look up at the stars," she said. "just remember that there's someone up there who loves you and is thinking of you. Will you do that for me, Benjamin?"

He looked deep into her eyes. "I promise."

After a moment of silence, Catalina turned and looked back at the stars. Her brown eyes filled with water. "Like diamonds in the sky," she whispered.

Benjamin reached into his pocket and pulled out a diamond ring. "Not exactly..." He tried to clear his throat, but it sounded more like a nervous groan. "I think this one may have fallen for you." Benjamin presented the ring to Catalina. It sparkled. "Catalina, will you..?"

"Yes," she said abruptly without giving it a second thought.

"Really? You will?" he said nervously.

"I thought you would never ask." She looked up at him and smiled softly.

"It's been on my mind for a long time."

All of a sudden, Catalina's eyes lowered and her smile was gone. She felt distraught and didn't know why. It might have been her own insecurities coming back to haunt her; or was it the mission. *But I don't know the outcome of it all, I just...*

She paused in thought. "Benjamin, there's a chance that I might not…"

Benjamin grabbed Catalina's chin so that she could face him. "I know. I've read the fine print," he began. "but that doesn't change the fact that I love everything about you." He paused. "The list goes on for days."

"You promise?" Catalina said.

He brushed the hair from her face and tucked it to the back of her ear. "You're the only one that I want to call my Party Doll."

Catalina looked into Benjamin's eyes, which were also filled with water. "I'll always be your Party Doll, Benjamin," she whispered, as she leaned up to kiss him.

-16-

Planet, Xissba.

M-33 Galaxy: Scorbic Star System.

The chamber doors opened and the two Noraphamara that stood to each side of the entry way kneeled with their heads bowed as Minda entered.

"The light shines grim upon the awakening of the second day," Carnmassicre said with his back turned. He was standing near one of the blood candles. He embraced the red flame as it flickered between his fingers and in his white eyes, at once turning them to an infectious pink. The flame was now a deeper shade of red than before. "Much blood has been spilled since Scorbic's star has risen," he said without expression.

"Much has been, my Prince," Minda said.

"And much more will come. Nevertheless, the era will commit to the suffering and it will not cease until the end has come to those who have refused the oath."

Carnmassicre relished the pain from his blistered fingers and for its affection, he drew them closer to the flame. "Mercy for the weak," he said with a hint of rage in his calm voice.

"What is your wish, my Prince?"

"Seed the clouds so that the storm will cover the planet, so the water saturates the soil."

"And when the others come?"

"Summon the Maradazza." Carnmassicre withdrew his fingers from the flame and then watched as the blisters vanished from his skin, leaving no trace of scaring or pain. "And they will grab mercy by the throat and crush the race that defies the Era." He waved the back of his hand. "You may go."

Minda lowered her head. "My Prince," she said, and then walked away.

A multitude of Rekluse swarmed the surface with their riders, the Sucturamara, clenching to the strapped harnesses as hundreds of pointed legs trampled over thousands of dead soldier's bodies. Chirps and pincher clacking overwhelmed the sounds of crushing bones as the Rekluse quickened their pace. The last remaining soldiers of the 16th Infantry ran for their lives, knowing they were overpowered and outmatched. They looked desperately for shelter, a foxhole, a landed ship, anything that would save them from what was chasing them, but there was nothing that fit those descriptions. There was a river that was about a quarter of a mile away, and at the other side there was what seamed to be a fenced-in base of some kind, but as they got closer to the riverbank, it was then identified as Camp Torpid.

When the soldiers reached the river, they had no other choice but to swim, and so they jumped. The Rekluse stopped dead in their tracks just before the land tied into the water. One of the Sucturamara dismounted from its Rekluse with its pointed tongue flickering. "NAABBA SOOLLIIBBA!" the beast cackled.

"Corporal, what did it say?" a soldier gasped.

"Sir," the corporal gasped, "the water's poisoned."

"Keep swimming, men," another soldier shouted from a distance.

"It's like swimming in molasses."

"It's the poison."

The soldiers had grown weaker with each stroke. Without remorse, the Sucturamara waited in silence as the soldiers drowned by the numbers. They didn't move until the last man was afloat and the painful yelling had stopped.

Through the event horizon, in the U.S.S. Mayflower.

After spending hours in a packed briefing room, the paratroopers of the 908th Airborne Division took some time for some R-N-R. Some raided the mess hall and attended movie night, while others retired to their quarters to pack their gear and prep for the mission. Eleven troopers from Aerie's company spent their time in launch bay 4 to make the best of what little they had. The bay was filled with forty-one mini shuttles and various cargo. It was the perfect place for the retreat.

Shortly after the others had arrived, Corporal Dix was the last to enter the bay with a half-smoked cigarette resting between his lips, a roughly worn out brown saxophone case in one hand, and an old black fedora that belonged to his grandfather in the other. He didn't say a word to the other soldiers when he entered, but nodded when they greeted him. Private First Class Todd,

Staff Sergeant Stephens, Specialist Jackson, Corporal Johnson, Private E-2 Molland, and Corporal Page carried on with their gambling as they sat around a crate with a half full bottle of Jack Daniels and six filled shot glasses. Half a deck of cards rested next to the bottle and money was scattered in piles. Private Lawson and Corporal Booster sat at a nearby crate playing a game of chess while they gambled for cigarettes. At a distance, Sergeant McDermott performed push-ups while First Class Seller sat on a crate with one leg bent and the other thrown over the edge, looking at an ex-fiancé's picture. Specialist Mayer slouched on a crate in a nearby corner, puffing on a freshly lit cigarette. He nodded at Dix.

Dix nodded back, and then sat the case and the fedora down on an empty crate. He took a drag from his cigarette, inhaled deeply and held the smoke in his lungs for a moment. He didn't pay any attention to the other soldiers' voices or what they were doing, he only paid attention to the sounds of a blues guitar, the base and a drum beat that played in a slow tempo in his head. He bobbed his head to the beat. Dix was now in his own little world. He opened the case and pulled out his recently shined sax, its mouthpiece and reed, while tapping his foot to the imaginary beat. He connected the two pieces and the reed together, then picked up his fedora and placed it on his head, tilting it to the side. He moistened the tip with his lips and began to play for an audience that only he could see.

"Seller, are you ever gonna put that picture away?" Molland said before gulping his shot.

"It's not healthy, you know."

"Bad habits die hard," Seller returned.

Mayer took a deep drag from his cigarette. "Was she any good?"

"What do you mean, any good?"

"He means sex, you love sick kid. So tell us. Was she any good in the sack or what?" Todd asked.

The other soldiers urged along with Todd, but Stephens was quiet as he shuffled cards.

"A good man never tells," Seller smiled.

"Rrrright," Johnson said sarcastically. "Every man tells, no matter what they say."

"This one doesn't," Seller returned.

A round of shots was poured and cards were dealt.

"Checkmate. You now owe me three smokes, Lawson," Booster said. "Face it, bud, you suck."

Lawson shook his head as he passed over his cigarettes. "I know. You don't have to tell me."

He counted the last remaining cigarettes in his pack and then looked up at Booster. "Double or nothing?"

Booster looked at his pile of cigarettes. "Do you have enough?"

"I'm good for it. You?"

"Loser sets board."

McDermott stopped at his hundredth push-up, and then continued his exercises with sit-ups. Even though he didn't contribute to any of the conversations, he enjoyed listening to them taunt each other. He had never smoked nor had a drop of liquor in his life. His comrades called him *"Health Nut McDermott,"* but he didn't mind. McDermott was proud of what he had: a strong physique, healthy lungs, and no bad habits except for one, which was war. That was his drug, his drive, and his excitement. He was the kind of guy that lived his life day-by-day, *and that was okay,* he told himself time and time again in the heat of battle. Still McDermott knew he had the worst habit in the room.

"I fold," Stephens said, and then poured the shot into his mouth.

"So do I," Molland said, and raised his shot glass.

Johnson shook his head and gulped; Jackson followed without saying a word. Todd and Page were now at a standoff.

"I raise you ten," Page said.

Todd placed a ten-dollar bill on the money pile then added two additional tens. "And I raise you twenty."

"You got it, money bags," Page returned.

Jackson looked at Todd. "You think that's a good idea?"

Todd nodded. "If you want to win big, you have to hand your balls to luck."

"So that Lady Luck can smash 'em with a hammer," Page said.

Molland shivered from the thought. "Ouch!" he painfully murmured.

Dix stopped playing; his eyes closed and he continued to nod to the music. After his rest, he resumed with a long high note. He sustained the high note for half a minute without taking any additional breaths. His eyes were still closed and he could hear applause from his imaginary audience.

"Three queens, pal," Todd said as he displayed his cards on the crate.

Page followed. "Full house, my man."

"Shit!"

"I'd say that ole' girl just put your balls in a sling,

cocked back to Brooklyn, and slammed the life right out of 'em," Molland chuckled.

"Now pay up and drink up, bud," Page said as he reached for the pile of money.

Lawson picked up a cigarette and was about to light it.

"I don't think so, bud," Booster said abruptly. "No smoking the merchandise."

Lawson sat back and examined the board. He then moved his knight and placed it into position. Booster picked up his bishop, then moved it diagonally to Lawson's rook and snatched the piece off the board. "Your king is fucked. You know that, right?"

"We'll see." Lawson looked at the board for a full two minutes, then retaliated by moving his queen diagonally to the left and took Booster's queen. "Checkmate! Ya, Bastard."

Booster examined the board to see if there was a way out, but there wasn't. He knew that, but didn't want to admit it, especially to himself. "I don't know what to say. I have never lost a game in my life."

"Well now you have." Lawson held out his hands and gave a sly smirk. "Pay up, Booster."

Even though Dix never took dedications, he played until his lips went numb and the mood was gone.

McDermott did one last sit-up.

The door beeped.

And beeped again.

"Come in," Max said.

As Sara was about to enter, she paused when she saw Max sitting on the floor with his legs crossed and his Ninja-to resting over them. "Sorry, I'll come back later."

"It's alright, come in."

Sara sat and crossed her legs before Max, and observed as he conducted his sword maintenance. "What's on your mind, girlie?" he asked, his eyes never leaving his weapon.

"I..." she began, paused, and then gave a slight smile of assurance. "I wanted to see you."

Max returned the smile, this time making eye contact with her. "How's your dad?"

"He's well," she replied.

"Good."

"Are you nervous?"

Max was somewhat surprised by her question, but didn't hesitate to answer. "I'm prepared for whatever may occur." He picked up the open bottle of clove oil and dabbed the liquid onto the folded cloth, and continued to polish the blade.

Sara stood up and walked towards the window and watched the white streaks of stars as they flowed like liquefied veins inside the wall of the event horizon. "I admire your courage, Max."

"I could say the same about you," he said.

"Why do you say that?"

"Why?" Max sheathed his sword and laid it in front of him. He then closed the bottle of clove oil and his cleaning kit, putting them both on the table behind him. Before approaching Sara, he placed the Ninja-to on his bed. "Because you had the guts to sneak into my ship and put yourself in harm's way."

"To tell you the truth, Max, I was frightened to

death and I had no idea what I was doing. I shouldn't have been there. I could have gotten us killed"

"You did what you had to do to save your father." He placed his hands on Sara's shoulders. "I would have done the same."

Sara reached for Max's hand and squeezed it. "I still don't have the words," she said. "but..." She looked up at him, kissed his cheek and hugged him. "…thank you."

Even though Max's arms were around Sara, he wasn't used to that type of affection, or any type of affection for that matter, since *Emily*. And even though Sara didn't know the mysteries of the troubled stranger who had come back into her life, she was able to feel the comfort and security of his embrace.

"You know, you're right," Max said.

"About what?" she asked.

"You're not a liability."

-17-

Max jumped up, awakened by another bad dream, but this time the dream was slightly different. Words from his wife's lips that were once deafening were now muted. He could no longer hear her scream, but he needed to. He needed to hear her.

He lay back down with his arm resting on his sweaty forehead. His eyes filled with tears and anger as the emptiness set in. He tried to hold back the tears but couldn't, and when he closed his eyes, he could remember hearing a whisper.

"*Her fingers bleed in vain* ," Then he saw Minda holding his unborn child in her blood-covered hands. Then the words crept from her lips, *"My gift to you, Widower."*

He didn't understand why, but that part never happened.

Is it telling me something? he thought over and over. Deep down he knew the answer to that question, but he didn't understand how.

Captain Teple sat in his chair with narrow eyes, his fingers tapping nervously at the edge of the armrest. However, he kept his composure as he gazed at the visual screen.

Commander Lawrence noticed Teple's discomfort from the corner of his eye and leaned towards him. "Is everything alright?" he whispered.

"I think so. I just have a bad feeling about what we might find when we reach Xissba," Teple said. "Ms. Manning, report status."

"Coast is clear, sir. We'll be reaching Xissba within two hours."

"Lieutenant, maintain course."

"Aye, Captain."

Teple turned to Lawrence. "Are all squadrons ready for deployment?"

"Just about, and the 908th division will be boarding the shuttles within the hour."

Teple nodded. "Ensign, any word from the 16th Infantry?"

"Not yet, sir." Ensign Lyy-Maau took a double-take at his panel. "Sir, I'm receiving their transmission now."

"Open."

The transmission was almost unrecognizable. Words were chopped with waves of static, as the com signal faded in and out. After three repeated fades into white noise, the transmission was severed by high pitch static.

"Ensign," Lawrence stood up, "did we lose it?"

Lyy-Maau nodded. "The transmission was sent twenty hours ago."

Lawrence and Teple turned to each other.

"Twenty hours? I think your bad feeling has just become a reality," Lawrence said.

"This isn't good," Teple returned.

"I agree."

"Lieutenant, go to impulse-3." Teple returned to Lawrence. "Inform Air-Captains Rook and McLachlan that the 908th will be dropping within the hour and so they need to meet with their squad and Colonel Wellington."

"Understood."

"And tell the priest to meet with both squads and the 908th for a quick prayer before deployment."

Lawrence nodded. "Aye, sir."

"Ensign, open a channel to all vessels." Teple adjusted himself in his chair then took a silent breath before transmission.

The door to briefing room number four slid open and Commander Lawrence and Jesuit G'nawa entered with their hands clasped before them. The alien priest's skin had a glossy blue tint to it. His eyes were an ocean blue that were as deep as they were kind. He wore a traditional holy robe that covered his six-foot-five stature, and wore a G'nawaian cross with a G'nawaian Christ on it.

"Commander. Father," Capt. McLachlan greeted.

G'nawa nodded. "Captain."

"I've asked Father G'nawa to meet with you for a prayer before going out into battle."

Lawrence told the squadron, "All yours, Father."

G'nawa stepped forward with his hands folded before him. He glanced at Captain McLachlan and the other pilots with gentle eyes, then bowed his head and began the Lord's Prayer.

When the prayer ended, G'nawa raised his head

and said, "May grace accompany you all as you face the enemy of peace."

"Thank you for your prayers, Father," Lawrence said.

G'nawa placed his hand on Lawrence's shoulder and looked deep into his eyes. "We need all the help we can get, Commander."

Lawrence nodded.

G'nawa squeezed his shoulder. "There are dark hours to come."

"Peace comes with a price, Father," Lawrence said.

"Yes, Commander," G'nawa said, and then walked out.

Capt. McLachlan and Lt. Broomfield were the last two pilots to leave the room. Broomfield saw Lawrence standing by the door with a look of anticipation. "I better let you go, Captain. I'll see you in an hour," she said, then lifted a brow and smiled at Lawrence. "Commander."

"Aye. Until then." McLachlan took an unnoticeable breath as she approached Lawrence.

"Commander."

"I want you to be..."

"I'm not the type of woman that uses sex to get what I want," McLachlan blurted. "You..." She paused and gave herself a mental slap for what she had just said. She didn't want to show her embarrassment, but her facial expression gave her away.

Lawrence was stunned and didn't know what to say, but two words, "I know."

McLachlan stuttered a bit before managing a clear sentence. "I-I'm sorry, Commander," she said, and then took a deep breath before continuing another sentence. "I think I'll shut up now and put me foot in me mouth."

"It's alright."

"It is?"

"Yeah, but only if you call me Anom."

McLachlan felt a little more at ease. "What were you saying?"

"I want you to be careful out there. And," he cracked a smile, "will you?"

"Aye."

"Come again, Captain?"

"I will. Join you for dinner, that is. And it's Rhiannon, if you feel comfortable with that." She lightly bit her bottom lip and smiled back. "But after all this, ye know."

"Great. Sounds good." Lawrence looked back before walking out. "By the way, do you play chess?"

"Sometimes with me sis. Why?"

"I think you could be a worthy opponent."

McLachlan gave Lawrence a competitive look. "Would you like to make a wager, Commander?"

Lawrence chuckled. "Like what?"

"Well, I'll need a sparing partner for a week. Wingman Yamaguti will be visiting her family when we return to Earth."

"Okay. And if I win?"

"You get a kiss."

Lawrence reached for her cheek. "I'll make sure to win," he said, while looking into her eyes.

She returned by cupping her hands over his. "No cheating. If I have to follow the rules, so do you," she said and stepped back to walk away.

"I promise. No cheating," he said.

"Till then," she said, and gave him a playful wink before turning away.

"Till then," he said, and watched her from a distance.

The door opened to Wingman William Chaz's quarters as Broomfield walked by.

"Eddie says hi," Chaz said.

Broomfield stopped, turned and saw Chaz with a big grin and his pet tarantula propped on his shoulder. "Disgusting creature," she said with a grimacing frown.

"Where's the love?" Chaz frowned.

"I'm sorry but, yuck."

"He needs love too, you know." He grabbed his eight-legged pet and held it with both hands.

"Awww, poor thing. He'll live," she said, and then started to walk away.

"Wait. Would you like to..."

"If you think I should mend that bug's broken heart with a kiss, think again."

"No, no, no. Would you like to join me for some chow? It gets lonely sometimes."

"Why didn't you join the others before?" She looked back and saw the sad puppy dog look on his face, and sighed. "Don't. I hate when you do that."

"Are you hungry?"

"A little, but..."

"Then let's go," he said. "It's bad luck to fly on an empty stomach."

"Speak for yourself, Chaz. I'll have some crackers and a juice. Play it safe, I say."

"Sounds good. Give me a minute to put Eddie in his cage and we'll head to the Mess."

"Good idea."

"Hull stop, Lieutenant," Teple said, and stood up from his chair.

"Aye, sir," Lt. Tuu-Maa said.

"Distance?"

"One hundred and sixty-four kilometers to Xissba's surface," Manning said.

Lawrence walked in. "What did I miss?"

Teple looked back. "It's time. Is everything taken care of?"

"Yes, sir."

"Good to hear, Commander."

"Captain, I'm reading heavy weather disturbances coming from the planet's atmosphere," Lieutenant Commander Miller announced.

"Where's it located on the planet, Lieutenant?"

"It's surrounding the globe, Captain."

"Magnify visual," Lawrence said.

Dark gray clouds hunched over Xissba without a trace of separation. They were thick, puffy and aggressive. The atmosphere lit up in all directions of the planet with sporadic flashing pops of bluish white thunder and winds reaching seventy-two miles an hour. In spots on the planet, clouds were slightly thinner, black and funneled with gusty winds upwards of a hundred miles an hour. Even though the clouds were swirled, the sensors didn't indicate any tornado activity anywhere on the surface.

Teple was puzzled from the discovery. He folded

his arms and tapped his finger on his chin, watching the screen in wonder.

"What do you think?" Lawrence asked.

"I don't know. It's odd."

"Should we launch a probe over the atmosphere?"

Teple shook his head. "I don't want to take any chances of detection. Lieutenant, what's the weather like on the surface?"

"Gusty winds, lighting showers, patchy fog, monsoon conditions, and heavy snow."

"Heavy snow, too," Teple said, returning his gaze to the screen.

"I think our boys are in for a long ride," Lawrence said.

"Ensign Tomms, get Colonel Wellington on the com and have him come to the bridge ASAP. I think he may want to see this."

"Aye, sir."

"And open all channels to the fleet."

"Understood."

Lawrence glanced at Sara and saw a look of worry. As she looked back at him, he knew what she was thinking. He gave a confident wink to ease her mind and to let her know that everything was going to be okay, and that Max would be fine... *at least for the time being,* he thought.

-18-

Troopers of the 908th Airborne Division waited in the shuttles for the order to deploy. There were ten troopers to a ship. Each was armed with a rifle that had three settings (single shot, three round burst, and full auto). The rifle also had a pulse grenade launcher connected underneath the barrel. They were also issued a sidearm. Both weapons were armed with armor-piercing rounds. Each trooper had six pulse grenades strapped to the sides of their chests, one boot knife, and one pair of Paral-Cuffs (to cause paralysis to the Noraphamara's nervous system). They were also geared with a susette bag that had four days worth of K-rations, a winter stocking cap, a pair of winter gloves, two fresh pairs of socks, a folding trench tool (an arm length shovel), and a machete (both strapped to their packs). Inside their packs were a box of waterproof matches, three flare sticks, and an aid-kit. And each man had a digital map, a mini mag-lite, two canteens, and a parachute pack with two back-up chutes. Some troopers had more to carry, at least for the jump-like flamethrowers (to burn the bodies of the dead Noraphamara or Rekluse), a com's device for those who were comsmen, and medical supplies for those who were the medics. As for cigarettes, the troopers had to supply their own... *the same could be said for courage.*

In shuttle five, Lieutenant Braga, Private Kallan, Private Lewis, Corporal Sagan, Seller, McDermott, Dix, Lawson, Todd, and Page may have been ready, but that didn't mean that they were emotionally prepared. At the far end of the shuttle, Dix had his pocket-size bible and read Psalm 91, while he tapped nervously on his rifle. *Thou shalt not be afraid for the terror by night; nor the arrow that flieth by day; nor for the pestilence that walketh in darkness...*

Across from Dix, Lewis turned to Kallan and saw his hands shake as Kallan tried to light a cigarette, while at the same time stopping himself from vomiting on his boots. It was both Lewis's and Kallan's first jump. New arrivals, *'Greenies'* the other troopers called them.

McDermott stared vacantly at the floor and squeezed a tennis ball. Ten squeezes later, he switched to the other hand.

Sagan didn't say much, maybe for an occasional allergenic cough or sniffle. At least he came prepared with drops for those dry itchy eyes.

Page pulled out another cigarette from his breast pocket. He flicked open his Zippo, lit the cigarette and inhaled deeply.

"Isn't that your fourth cigarette?" Todd asked.

"It takes the edge off," Page said, while exhaling the smoke into the air.

Todd shook his head with a slight nasal chuckle. "To each his own, I guess."

"To each his own," Lawson said after popping his chewing gum.

Todd turned to see what Lieutenant Braga was up to, and was curious as to why it was taking so long for the okay. He saw Braga nod his head at the shuttle pilots as they were whispering to each other. Todd looked at Page. "What do you think is taking so long?"

"How should I know? Maybe they're having trouble with the shuttles, or maybe the bay doors are stuck," he said.

"Funny, Page," he said. "What do you think they're whispering about? What's so important that they couldn't share it with us?"

Page depleted his cigarette before extinguishing it on the sole of his boot. "I don't know. If you feel so troubled about it, ask the lieutenant."

Todd returned to Braga's direction. "Lieutenant, what's the holdup?"

Braga looked back. "We're waiting for the ships to reach orbit. Then the bombers will attack, and then we'll go. Will there be anything else, Private?"

"No, sir. Understood, sir."

"Good," Braga nodded. "I'll inform you when it's time."

Todd looked at his watch then leaned his head back and took a deep breath to calm the pre-jump jitters. The troopers didn't have much to say to one another, so they kept to themselves, their minds wandering, and the inner hull of the shuttle was quiet from then on. Only the sound of idling engines remained.

An hour and fifteen minutes later, the launch bay doors opened and the cloud-covered planet was in plain view. *No sign of Demonixa. But was that a good sign?*

Braga looked at his troopers and gave a confident

nod. “It’s time,” he said. “Buckle up, Men. We’re in for a rough ride.”

Thrusters engaged. One after the other, the shuttles poured out of the Mayflower and the Aurora like mad hornets, and were escorted by seven Typhoon Migs that led the way into obit. There were eighty-four shuttles in all, with eight hundred and forty troopers preparing themselves for the rough descend through Xissba’s orbit. Even though it was most of the troopers’ fifth drop, it seemed like the first. *It always felt like the first time.* As for the *Greenies*, most of them closed their eyes and hoped for the best. Some struggled to hold themselves together by covering their mouths to keep from puking, but that didn’t work.

The shuttles shook from heavy turbulence. The friction was just about unbearable to the shuttle pilots, but they managed to maintain control of their spacecraft. *It was a roller coaster ride from hell, and the ride was far from over.*

Before entering deep orbit, Migs went into formation by surrounding the shuttles from all sides; one at the lead, two on the right flank and two on the other, and two at the rear. Seconds later they reached the upper atmosphere and entered the thick blinding clouds.

Even though the heavy turbulence subsided to a mild tremble from the shockwaves of nearby lightning strikes and gusting winds hammering the surface below, there were other things to worry about. God-awful things.

The enemy is near.

They know we’re here.

And a new breed of evil awaits.

When the clouds came to an end, the rain poured in thick beads of tears, as if the universe was crying. Black smoke hovered from smoldering bombarded areas, causing pore visibility. Without any warning, enemy fire pierced the smoke. Migs blindly returned fire.

"Are you're censors working?" a Mig pilot asked another.

"Negative. They must be jamming us."

"Rita-1 to all Migs. The weather's scrambling your censors. Bombardiers and Halo squadrons disbanded all airwave threats prior to your arrival. Do you copy?"

"We copy, Rita-1," the lead Mig pilot returned. "What is your current status, Halo?"

"We have minor casualties, but the Bombardiers have sustained heavy damage."

"Is there any chance you could give us some air support? Copy."

"We'll do what we can."

As the Migs and shuttles came closer to clearing the elevated smoke, the Demonixa intensified their defense by thickening their fire, which seemed to be coming from all directions. When they reached visibility, the left rear Mig was the first to be hit. The wing was shredded and began to fold, and the right thruster ceased, then reversed polarity causing the small craft to spiral out of control and into the nearest shuttle. The two ships collided and were both shot back by the forceful impact, whirling down to the surface in one large ball of flame. The rear shuttles had to swerve out of the way to avoid the deadly collision. But as one of the shuttles tried to swerve into safety, a lightning bolt struck the ship's thrusters, causing the rear coolant tank to rupture and the inner hull to engulf in flames. Screams could be heard coming from the shuttle as it fell.

Loud thumps from nearby explosions shook the shuttle's hull to where the ship's walls felt like they were about to crack open. No one could hear themselves think or breathe, but they could sure feel their hearts pound like scared rabbits. Braga stood up and braced himself with a firm grip on a bar that was located next to the door.

"Hook check!" he shouted.

The troopers stood up and hooked themselves on the static line, just above their heads and double-checked each other's gear.

"Ten ready!"

"Nine ready!"

"Eight ready!"

"Seven ready!"

"Six ready!"

"Five ready!"

"Four ready!"

"Three ready!"

"Two ready!"

"One ready!" Braga ended.

"Lieutenant!" the copilot called. "We have a problem, sir!"

"What is it?"

"The wind speed is at 102 mph at drop altitude, sir! We're gonna have to descend to five hundred feet!"

"Fuck," Braga murmured to himself. "What's the wind speed at five hundred?"

"Seventy-five mph, give or take, sir!"

"We have no other choice!" Braga turned and looked at his troopers and saw the adrenaline in their eyes.

Page nodded to Braga. "Just give the word, Lieutenant!"

The shuttle trembled from a nearby explosion, but this time the vibration was even more destructive. Seller and Sagan looked out a window and saw one of the shuttles split in two as all its troopers spilled out.

"Shit! Did you see that?" Sagan blurted.

"Yeah!" Seller returned in shock.

One of the windows shattered and four others cracked from the shock wave. The troopers turned to cover their faces.

"CHRIST, MY HAND!" Lawson shouted in stinging pain.

Soon after, inner shields automatically sealed all the windows.

Page looked back and grabbed Lawson's hand and quickly picked out the little shards of glass.

"There's no permanent damage! You'll be fine!" He then pulled out a bandage from his aid-kit and wrapped and tied it to the mildly lacerated hand.

"It might not be bad, but it hurts like a son-of-a-bitch!"

"But your guts aren't gonna come out!"

"Thanks for the comfort, Doc!"

"TEN SECONDS!" Braga shouted.

The shuttle took an enemy round at the mid-section of its hull, which went strait through the floor and out the roof. No one was hit, but the aftershock was there. Then another round penetrated through, but this time the copilot was hit in the head, then the round went through the side of the hull, missing the pilot and Braga.

Braga ducked before the round could hit him. "THREE SECONDS!" he shouted.

The pilot turned to his copilot and saw that half of his head was missing and the other half of his skull was starting to dissolve. The pilot watched in shock as the bones liquefied and the skin collapsed and slumped onto the copilot's shoulder.

"Jesus Christ!" the pilot screamed. He quickly turned back and saw that he was about to collide with another shuttle. He jerked the ship to the right, then to the left. As the pilot tried to regain control, he succumbed to two rounds; one to his arm and the other to his chest. He slumped forward causing the shuttle to nosedive. The troopers struggled to maintain their balance. Braga unhooked himself from the static line then reached over to the console and pushed the button to activate the green light to open the door.

Braga reattached himself back to the static line and grabbed the edge of the opened door.

"GIVE 'EM HELL, MEN!" he shouted, and was the first to drop.

The enemy is near.

They know we're here.

And a new breed of evil awaits.

God-awful things...

TwilightS In ThE SkY

"When I get to heaven to St. Peter I will tell one more soldier reporting, Sir, I've served my time in hell."

-A soldier's prayer
WWII, June 6, 1944 D-DAY

-1-

Planet, Xissba.
M-33 Galaxy: Scorbic Star System.

DAY ONE

"MEDIC!" A voice screamed from within the midst of the monsoon rain.

Within the thick beads and smoke, enemy rounds buzzed passed, as troopers who survived the drop dived to the saturated ground. The aggressive weather and weapon fire consumed the drop zone, making it hard to communicate. As one trooper looked up to the deep grey sky, he could see light behind the remaining parachuters. E*xplosions*? *Or lightning*? He thought.

"Randle, can you see?" One Trooper asked.

Privet Randle turned away from the clouds and peaked above the crown of the rock where he was standing. "I can't see. The rain is too thick." He quickly ducked as an enemy round hit and recessed into the front of the rock. "SHIT!" he groaned as he dropped for cover. He looked again. "Sweet Jesus…"

"What is it?"

"Quick… look."

The trooper crawled to where Randle was standing, stood up and saw what looked like the living end. *The God awful thing.*

"THEIR COMING!" Another trooper shouted.

"NAACCTTUUR NAASSHHMMIIK!" The commanding Maradazza roared.

The rampage begun and the enemy fire intensified when the commands were made. The Maradazza rumbled into the fog of war like the demolition of death that they were. Water splashed off them that made the blackness of their carapace shimmer, and the florescent blotches accented their blood rank. Unlike their counterpart, the Sucturamara, the Maradazza had red blotches and wielded a bio-neurotoxin rifle. When in contact, the round would burst inside the body and dissolve everything within its bull's eye radius.

"Stay down, and you won't get hit!"

"Watch the East and West flanks!" Braga said.

"Keep firing!"

When the Maradazza came close enough to a hand-to-hand battle, the troopers used and did what ever it took to stay alive. It took at least two troopers for one Maradazza and even then, they were too strong for a mere mortal.

"Does anyone know where Colonel Willington is?" Barga asked.

"No, Sir, I…"

Braga continued to fire until the magazine was empty. "Try coms, Corporal." he said while reload his rifle.

"Yes, Sir."

There was no time to think, just react as the rounds and the rushing bulking mass advanced.

"Jesus Christ." Randle said, holding his boot knife with a trembling hand, while waiting for the Maradazza that was running towards him.

Full of adrenaline, Randle thrust his knife into the creature's abdomen but only the hilt was showing. The creature wheezed and backhanded Randle in the face, knocking his helmet off. The young trooper was slightly dazed and tried to shake it off before the Maradazza's next attack. When Randle's eyes came into focus, the creature pulled the blade from its wound with a screech that pierced the trooper's ears. After discarding the knife, the Maradazza aimed its rifle at its enemy. Yet before the creature could pull the trigger, another trooper ran in with the butt of his rifle in the air as a distraction. The creature switched targets and fired. The trooper flew back with his chest open and his insides dissolved.

With the creature's back turned, Randle pulled out his side arm and fired at it until there was nothing left but a click. The Maradazza dropped its rifle and fell lifeless to the ground.

Elsewhere on the battleground, an unfortunate trooper was sprawled screaming for his mother, as two medics desperately tried to retrieve his internal organs.

"It's no use. Move on." The medic said to the other.

"Medic!" Another trooper called.

"Where is he?" The medic asked the other.

"Just follow the voice!"

With the wide spread of troopers landing it was hard to make the drop zone by just dropping; they had to manipulate the guiding handles on their parachutes to maneuver out of the way of enemy fire. Some were not as successful and landed miles away from the goal, but lived. Others were not as fortunate, and were dead before their boots ever touched the ground.

The wind blew with a forceful whistle and the sky fell like a Louisiana rain… but it had no resemblance of home, but a nightmare that would never end.

…and if I am awake, I am in Hell.

A trooper wandered in a dazed shock, looking for his arm, while mumbling a lullaby that his mother hummed to him when he was a child. Even though he was moving well for having a severed limb, he was utterly oblivious to what was happening around him. Nevertheless, that lullaby… might ease the thought of dieing.

As the last of the shuttles lifted into the clouds and out of orbit, the thunder and lightning stopped and the winds calmed. But the thick rain remained.

The smoke had arisen and the fog of war was overwhelming. There was the smell of sulfur and the taste of blood. Their blood; the God-awful things' blood. This was the peril of liberation. Hell waited… and with it death.

Forty miles to the west of the battle, McDermott crouched into the brush of weeds as he quickly cut himself free from the straps that were connected to his parachute. He looked up to see if there were any others who would have landed near his drop point, but only saw Page struggling to cut free from his straps.

"Damn straps!"

"Shhhhhhh." I'll be right there."

Once free from the straps, Page searched desperately for his medical supplies. "Shit! This isn't good." he said, while rubbing his face nervously.

"What's the matter?"

"I lost most of my gear in the drop. Damn!"

"Just be grateful that you still have you're rifle and side arm. We might be able to find something along the way."

"Now I just have enough for a half ass patch work."

Suddenly they heard a sound of crushing brush. The two troopers dropped and aimed their rifles at the direction of what ever was coming.

"Raven!" McDermott said in a raised whisper.

However, there was no response.

"I said raven!"

When the brush was loud enough to make contact a young trooper fell to the ground and coughed for air. "On the shoulder! Raven on the shoulder!"

McDermott and Page lowered their weapons and helped the young trooper to his feet.

"Is there anyone else with you?" Page asked.

"No." The trooper said in a huff. "I just landed about twenty minutes ago."

"About how far?" McDermott asked.

"Well." The trooper looked back and tried to estimate his distance. "I reckon two or thee miles give or take." He pulled out his canteen and took two big gulps. "I've been dodging the Marardazza all this time."

"What's your name, Corporal?" McDermott asked.

"Jason Bott, sir, from third company."

Later on, Page tapped his compass to make it work, but it was a battle that he could not win. “Damn thing.”

“If it didn’t work a mile back it’s not going to work now.” Bott said with a deep inhale from his cigarette.

“Thanks for the info. Smart ass.”

“Get down.” McDermott said.

“What is it?” Page asked.

“What does that look like to you?”

Bott pulled out his binoculars from its pouch.

“Is that someone hanging from a tree?” Page asked.

“What do you see?” McDermott asked.

“The overcast is a bit thick but… he’s moving.” Bott said.

The troopers cautiously ran towards the hanging soldier. When they arrived, he drew his rifle at them.

“Don’t shoot!” Bott said.

The hanging trooper withdrew. “Get me the hell down from here.” he said.

“Where’s you’re knife?” Page asked.

“I dropped it on the ground.”

“Hold on.” Before McDermott could cut the trooper down, faint chirping sounds echoed in the wind from within the fog. Through the trees and up ahead, the reverberations of a band of creepy-crawlies charged closer.

“Get the fuck down!” Page said.

Nothing yet.

“Rekluse.”

More chirps.

“Shit! Don’t leave me here like this.” The trooper begged.

Closer.

"Just play dead and you'll be fine." McDermott said.

Louder.

"What? Have you been drinking your own bath water? Get me the…"

Silence.

"Shhhhhhhh, don't breathe." Page said.

Out from the fog and into sight, the Rekluse appeared. The troopers shuddered, but knew better then to move. One of the Sucturamara spotted the hanging trooper and pulled back its beast, and then nudged it towards the suspended meat. When it got close enough, the Sucturamara hopped off the giant spider's back and inhaled deep to get the trooper's scent. The trooper held his breath and tried to stop his hands from shaking. Maybe that was enough; maybe that wasn't.

But as luck would have it, a few yards away, the commanding Sucturamara turned its head and stopped, noticing that one of its riders was distracted. "KIICCKKAA DIMMA!" It commanded.

The subordinate Sucturamara turned its head toward the direction of its commander, then back at the trooper, hissing before hopping on its Rekluse. It left the body hanging to rejoin the herd.

Bott, McDermott, and Page exhaled anxiously when the area had cleared.

"It's clear." Page said.

The hanging trooper opened one eye and exhaled forcefully when he knew for sure. "Christ all mighty! Get me down."

"Hold tight." McDermott said and began to cut.

"I feel like a Goddamned tea beg."

"What's you're name, Privet?" McDermott asked.

"Daaa..." The trooper said as he dropped to the ground.

"What was that?"

The trooper stood up. "David Mills!" he said while brushing himself off.

"From Fourth company?"

"No, sir. Eighth."

"I'm McDermott, and behind me are Corporal Bott and Corporal Page."

"Just call me Doc." Page said.

Mills nodded.

"They must be heading towards the battle."

"So to the south? Or is it south-east?" Page said.

"I don't know." Bott tapped his compass. "I have no idea. It's not working. Now what?"

"We keep our distance and follow them." McDermott said.

Lieutenant Braga and Corporal Booster supplied cover fire, as Private Mulland dove into the foxhole where the two troopers were. Mulland coughed and wheezed when he hit the ground. "Ca... can't breathe." He said as he struggled for air.

"Stay down and catch you're breath." Braga said, while replacing his magazine. "Does anyone know where McDermott, Page, Dix, Seller, Mayer?" He cocked his weapon and fired.

"No!" A trooper shouted. "Has anyone seen Dillon or Bott?"

"Dillon here." He said.

"Bott!"

Booster and Braga ducked as enemy fire buzzed by, grazing Booster's helmet. "Holy fuck! They got me! They got me!"

Braga skimmed his finger over the graze. "It's good."

"That was a close one." Booster said.

"Medic!" A trooper called.

Mulland picked up his helmet and put it on. "I think I pissed myself."

"It's the least of you're worries." Booster giggled.

"They're coming!" A trooper yelled.

"Coms! We need air support!"

Like sacks of flesh along the battleground, bodies' muddled in grotesque form, as the Maradazza scuttled closer to their enemy. Blood and liquefied bone marrow spewed out, just as the skin gave way at the limbs. Yet troopers could hear screams coming from what they thought were the dead.

Then again, were they really dead?

"Keep firing!"

"Watch the right flank!"

"Do what ever it takes to get them down! Don't let them through!"

"Medic!" Another trooper yelled.

From all sides they were coming closer… and closer.

If one were to look beneath and beyond the smoke and the cold beads of precipitation. One would see an irrevocable loss of life. One would believe in the roar of the battle cry, the chatter of the hungry beasts and the screams of my fallen brothers.

We are in hell together; in the beginning of what some have come to believe is the end.

At first, I did not understand what they meant when they said, "If you want peace, prepare for war and the price for freedom is blood." Now I truly know what it means.

Nevertheless, to those back on Earth who question why we are here, know that we may never make it home to give you an answer. Even so, I give my life to those who need it and that is my calling... and I would give my life to save a thousand more. That is my oath.

Printed in the United States
203448BV00001B/1-51/P